THE
EMPEROR'S
RiDDLE

THE EMPEROR'S RIDDLE

KAT ZHANG

Aladdin

NEW YORK LONDON TORONTO SYDNEY NEW DELHI

This book is a work of fiction. Any references to historical events, real people, or real places are used fictitiously. Other names, characters, places, and events are products of the author's imagination, and any resemblance to actual events or places or persons, living or dead, is entirely coincidental.

ALADDIN

An imprint of Simon & Schuster Children's Publishing Division
1230 Avenue of the Americas, New York, New York 10020
First Aladdin hardcover edition May 2017
Text copyright © 2017 by Cathy Zhang
Interior maps illustrated by Robyn Ng copyright © 2017 by Simon & Schuster, Inc.
Jacket illustration copyright © 2017 by Jim Tierney

For information about special discounts for bulk purchases,
please contact Simon & Schuster Special Sales at 1-866-506-1949
or business@simonandschuster.com.
The Simon & Schuster Speakers Bureau can bring authors to your live event.
For more information or to book an event contact the Simon & Schuster Speakers
Bureau at 1-866-248-3049 or visit our website at www.simonspeakers.com.
Jacket designed by Jessica Handelman
Interior designed by Mike Rosamilia
The text of this book was set in Weiss Std.
Manufactured in the United States of America 0317 FFG
2 4 6 8 10 9 7 5 3 1
Library of Congress Cataloging-in-Publication Data
Names: Zhang, Kat, 1991-
Title: The emperor's riddle / by Kat Zhang.
Description: First Aladdin hardcover edition. | New York : Aladdin, 2017. |
Summary: During a family trip to China, eleven-year-old Mia Chen and her
older brother, Jake, follow clues and solve riddles in hopes of finding
their missing Aunt Lin and, perhaps, a legendary treasure.
Identifiers: LCCN 2016027523 | ISBN 9781481478625 (hc) |
ISBN 9781481478649 (eBook)
Subjects: | CYAC: Adventure and adventurers—Fiction. | Buried treasure—
Fiction. | Missing persons—Fiction. | Family life—China—Fiction. | China—
Fiction. | BISAC: JUVENILE FICTION / Action & Adventure / General. |
JUVENILE FICTION / Family / Multigenerational. |
JUVENILE FICTION / People & Places / Asia.
Classification: LCC PZ7.Z454 Emp 2017 | DDC [Fic]—dc23
LC record available at https://lccn.loc.gov/2016027523

To Jenny and Renée,
A month apart would be too long

THE
EMPEROR'S
RiDDLE

1

DEEP IN THE CLOSET OF THE MASTER BEDROOM,
buried beneath piles of winter blankets and heavy coats,
was an old leather trunk. It might have been bright red
once upon a time. But the years had patched it with stains
and lighter portions where the leather had worn away.

Mia helped Aunt Lin lug the trunk from the closet,
each of them grabbing a dark metal handle. The trunk
was heavier than it looked, and Mia was already noodle-
armed from jet lag. She'd arrived in China less than
twenty-four hours ago, and most of that time had been
spent in transit—taking the train from Shanghai to
Fuzhou, and then the taxi here, to this apartment. Her
eyes kept slipping shut, trying to remind her that while

it was midafternoon in Fuzhou, it was the middle of the night back in America.

Once the trunk was out in the open, Mia saw that it was nearly large enough for her to climb inside. An image came to her—a snapshot of her curled in the trunk like a sleeping fairy, waiting for someone to wake her. Or maybe bound like a prisoner, straining at the rope around her wrists. That was the more exciting story, the kind Mia usually liked. But right now, sleeping for a hundred years sounded like the better option.

"Lost in your head again?" Aunt Lin smiled and brushed a strand of hair from Mia's face, bringing her back from her imaginings. "Come, let's see what's in this thing."

She rummaged around the nightstand until she produced an ancient-looking key. Mia was surprised her aunt still knew her way around. Aunt Lin and Mia's mother had grown up in this apartment, but it had been years and years since they'd been here last.

Mia had expected them to feel like she did—a puzzle piece that didn't fit.

Glum again, she pulled her knees against her chest. This month-long visit to China was supposed to be a

Great Opportunity for Mia and her older brother, Jake, to see where their family had come from. The last time they'd visited, Mia had been so little she barely remembered it.

You loved it, Mia's mother had said. *You had so much fun.*

But back then, Mia hadn't met Thea and Lizbeth yet. She hadn't cared that the trip would rip her from home for a third of summer vacation. The three of them hadn't spent a summer apart in years. Mia would make it back just in time to celebrate her twelfth birthday, but that wasn't much consolation.

A month was a long time to be apart from your best friends.

Anything might happen.

Aunt Lin sat and tucked an arm around Mia so they sloped against each other. "Do you want to open it?" she said, holding out the key. She grinned, like they were explorers—or maybe adventurous archaeologists, having just unearthed a treasure. She knew how much Mia enjoyed mysteries.

The lock turned with a satisfying *click*. Mia opened the lid slowly and peeked inside.

The first thing she saw was a big, square book. It

wasn't until she laid it open in her lap that she realized it wasn't a book at all, but a photo album. Inside, the photos weren't slipped into plastic pockets, but pasted onto black paper pages, like a scrapbook.

"Can you recognize your mother and me in any of those?" Aunt Lin said. She was lifting other things out of the trunk—a small frame of embroidered silk, a slender, cloth-wrapped vase. For a minute, Mia was too distracted to look at the album.

But she couldn't keep her eyes away for long. She squinted at each picture. Some were tiny, barely bigger than a postage stamp. Others were the size of her palm. All were black-and-white, though a couple looked like someone had tried to color them in afterward and hadn't done a very good job.

"That's Mom," Mia said, pointing at a family photo.

Her mother and Aunt Lin bookended a collection of four children, Aunt Lin the eldest, Mia's mother the baby. In the photograph, all four siblings gathered in a solemn huddle around the seated forms of Mia's late grandmother and grandfather. Her mother was barely more than a toddler, but she had the same sweet, round face she had now.

"And that's you, with the braids." This time, Mia pointed at the eldest child. The girl was maybe fourteen— around Jake's age. There was a familiar glint in her dark eyes, as if she were thinking of a joke.

On the next page, Mia found a picture of just the two of them—her mother and Aunt Lin holding hands and laughing at the camera. This time her mom looked to be four or five.

"That was the first day of my senior year of high school," Aunt Lin said. "One of your grandmother's friends borrowed a camera from someone."

She smiled and took the photo album in her careful, life-weathered hands. "Life-weathered" was a term Mia had learned from Aunt Lin, since no one but Aunt Lin used it. Her aunt liked to mash English words together, or substitute one word in a common phrase for another that suited her better. *You understand what I mean*, she'd say, and Mia always did.

The two of them weren't like the rest of the people in Mia's little family. They weren't like Mia's mom, who was always punctual, and loved to-do lists, and never let her thoughts wander off when they were supposed to be pinned down. They weren't like Jake, who did well in school without even trying, who always had people inviting him over to play basketball, or soccer, or tennis.

They weren't like Mia's dad, who'd left one day when Mia was little and never came back.

They were only like each other. *Cotton-candy-headed*, as Mia's mom sometimes teased; *Weird*, as Jake always complained. They loved stories and history and make-believe— and the exciting places where those things blurred into one another.

"Look," Aunt Lin said. "This is a picture of me during the Chinese New Year. I was nineteen—it was my first time home after being sent down to the countryside."

Mia studied the picture. It was hard to tell in the black-and-white photo, but her aunt looked heavily tanned. Her hair was still in braids, her smile secret and winking.

When a younger Mia had first heard her aunt's stories about her years in the countryside, she'd thought they sounded pretty exciting. Mia didn't have a head for school. She daydreamed through math and English classes alike, distracted by every passing noise in the hallway. Her teachers were always telling her to sit still, to keep her eyes forward.

To think about something that wasn't fantasy.

She thought she would have preferred tramping around outdoors every day, planting baby rice shoots, or hand-making bricks, or threshing wheat. She'd helped out at Thea's horse barn before, and that had been fun, the two of them giggling through their tasks and getting straw in their hair.

But she knew Aunt Lin had wanted to go straight to university after high school. She'd dreamed of becoming a history professor—not of being stuck doing farm work in rural China. She'd been there nearly three years before being allowed to come home again. Only then had she applied for university.

"Were you homesick?" Mia said. "When you were down in the country?"

"Of course," Aunt Lin said. "I missed my old friends. I missed my family—especially your mother! She was my little darling."

Mia always felt funny when she tried to think of her mother as a child—small enough to be someone's little darling. She was so grown up now.

"Ah! Here it is." Aunt Lin had gotten to the bottom of the trunk, and she lifted something swathed in layers of cloth. Mia pressed closer as her aunt undid the wrappings.

It was a Chinese brush painting of two black-and-white cranes. One had its wings lifted wide, as if in a dance. The other stared at the sky, its long neck curved in a sinuous S. Both bore a flash of red at the crowns of their delicate heads. Behind them stretched a rolling landscape of mountain peaks and valleys, cut through by a winding stream.

Aunt Lin sat back on her knees, the painting in her lap. "I haven't seen this in a long, long time. It was your grandmother's favorite painting. She used to hang it in her bedroom, right there—" She pointed to an empty spot on the wall by the closet door. "That way, she could see it every morning when she got out of bed."

Mia's grandparents had passed away long ago. She'd never even met them. Sometimes her mother or Aunt Lin would bring them up—say things like, *Oh, remember what Mom used to do?* or *Dad always liked those,* but mostly, Mia's grandparents were a mystery to her. The majority of her extended family was.

She tried to picture the woman her grandmother had been once upon a time. Someone who'd loved these dainty cranes so much she'd hung them in her bedroom. Someone who'd breathed and hummed and walked through this apartment, her feet pressed against the same floors Mia sat on now.

"Did Uncle take the painting down after she died?" Mia asked. Only her uncle still lived in this apartment. Aunt Lin and Mia's mother had moved to the United States long ago, and their remaining sister lived hours away, in another city.

Aunt Lin shook her head. "Your grandmother took it down herself. I think I was in middle school then, or maybe high school. This painting is a family heirloom— it's very old and very precious. It's a piece of history."

"Was she afraid someone would break it?"

There was a beat of silence before Aunt Lin answered. "There was a time when no one in China wanted any-thing to do with things that were old, and precious, and pieces of history," she said. "Or if they did—they kept quiet about it."

The room grew still. Mia got the shivery, unsettled feeling she always did when her aunt's mood dipped. Aunt Lin was seldom sad, but when she did get that way, it felt like doors closing in Mia's face. Like her aunt withdrew somewhere deep inside herself, where Mia couldn't follow.

Mia hated that more than anything. Even more than when Aunt Lin got overly excited about something and wandered off. At least then Mia could think of her aunt as a daredevil traveler—a swashbuckling heroine like those in Mia's favorite books. Besides, Aunt Lin always warned Mia before leaving on one of her sudden journeys, even if she forgot to tell anyone else.

The one time she hadn't, Mia had cried every day Aunt Lin was gone. *Your aunt has always been like this*, her mother had said in an attempt to comfort her. *She gets hooked by something—a new exhibition on tombs, a talk about ancient kings—and forgets everything else. Don't worry. She always finds her way back.*

But this had happened only months after Mia's parents had divorced; Mia had been very little. She hadn't believed that anyone who'd leave so abruptly would come home again.

Once she returned a few days later, Aunt Lin had sworn up and down that she'd never again take off without leaving Mia a message. That she'd never be gone when Mia needed her.

In all the years since, she'd never broken that promise.

Mia rested her chin against her aunt's shoulder and racked her brain for something—anything—helpful to say. Something that would bring her aunt back to her. "Can we take the painting with us when we leave? If your brother doesn't want it? You could hang it in your bedroom at home."

To her relief, Aunt Lin laughed. "Maybe we can. But it's far too early to talk about leaving—we've only just arrived. Did you want to see where my school used to be? Or the park where your mother liked to play when she was little?"

Mia just hugged Aunt Lin even tighter. "Will you take me?"

"Of course," Aunt Lin said. She kissed the top of Mia's head. "We're going to spend this whole trip together. I promise."

2

SOMETHING ELSE FROM AUNT LIN'S PAST SHOWED up later that afternoon: not a painting, but a man. He was powerfully built, his shoulders so broad they barely fit through the door, his fists as solid as oak. Despite his size, he seemed to take up very little room. Even less than Mia's uncle, who boisterously ushered him into the apartment and called out, "Sis, look who's come to see you!"

Mia's mom had left to buy groceries. Mia and Jake sat sprawled on the couch, trying to understand a Chinese historical drama, because Jake refused to watch cartoons. Their uncle caught Mia's eye and grinned. Mia looked away, her mouth forgetting how to smile back.

She and her uncle had met once, the last time Mia had visited China. But really, they were strangers. The man didn't *seem* like he should be intimidating—he had a soft, roundish feeling about him, like a laughing Buddha statue come to life. And so far, he'd been nothing but nice to Mia.

But still.

She'd never had an uncle before. He'd always *existed*, of course. But it was one thing to be home and know that a nebulous uncle lived across the ocean. It was a whole other matter to stay here with him. To see the way her mother and Aunt Lin chatted with him and laughed with him and seemed to expect Mia to do the same. As if she could just turn on some "family" switch inside her and pretend she'd known him her whole life.

Well, she couldn't. She avoided him, uncertain how to treat family who didn't feel like family.

Aunt Lin hurried out of her bedroom, her arms full of half-unpacked clothing. When she saw their visitor, she seemed so shocked she almost dropped all her blouses.

"*Ying*," she said.

Mia and Jake looked at each other. Even Jake had heard enough of Aunt Lin's stories to know about Ying—or the boy Ying had been, once, when Aunt Lin had been a girl. Like Aunt Lin, he'd shipped off to China's countryside on government orders after high school. The two of them had ended up at the same village. There, they'd become close friends—for a time.

As far as Mia knew, they hadn't parted on good terms.

But Aunt Lin looked happy to see him now. Ying's smile back was barely a smile at all—more like an unpracticed twitch of his lips. His fingers fidgeted at his sides. Mia's stranger-uncle excused himself to put the kettle on for tea, and beckoned for Jake to help him.

Which left Mia alone with Aunt Lin and Ying.

"She looks like you," Ying said, his gaze resting on Mia. His heavily lidded, downturned eyes made him look tired and dreamy. Unlike Mia's stranger-uncle, he still boasted a thick head of wavy hair. It puffed like a black cloud above his face.

He loomed over Aunt Lin, who was a small woman—several inches shorter than Mia's mother and nearly a whole head shorter than Jake. Only Mia remained smaller still.

Aunt Lin hugged Mia sideways against her. "She looks even more like her mother."

"Does she speak Chinese?" Ying said.

Mia's feathers ruffled. She'd gone to Chinese school every Saturday since she was four years old. She'd memorized the characters, and practiced reading from the textbooks, and she was more fluent, certainly, than Jake, who'd decided when he was ten that he no longer wanted to go. He wanted his Saturday mornings free for basketball and sleeping in.

Mia understood. In the United States, Chinese sometimes seemed like a burden. An extra rock she had to drag around when none of her friends needed to. But right now, staring up at Ying, those years of classes suddenly seemed like a badge of pride.

"Yes, I can," she said, a little huffily. "How do you do?"

Aunt Lin laughed. Ying just looked down at Mia. This time, his mouth didn't even twitch.

"Come, sit down," Aunt Lin said quickly.

While they moved to the table, Mia slipped her aunt a glance behind Ying's back. It was an *I don't know about him* sort of glance. She couldn't imagine a dour, solemn man like this ever being close with Aunt Lin. It was like asking a hummingbird to befriend an oil slick. But Aunt Lin just smiled back at Mia. *Don't worry,* she seemed to say. *He's all right.*

Mia wasn't so sure. She perched herself next to Aunt Lin at the table, so they faced Ying together.

At first their conversation was boring—a lot of *How have you been?* and *It's been so long* and *When did you move so close by?* Aunt Lin asked after Ying's family, and he asked after hers. They spoke of Ying's wife, whom Aunt Lin had never met. She teased that Ying should have brought her, then grew solemn when Ying admitted that the woman was ill and not doing well.

Finally, talk turned toward the years Aunt Lin and Ying had spent in the remote Fujian village. The two reminisced about waking up to roosters crowing and sleeping on straw-stuffed mattresses.

"Do you remember," Ying said casually, "our treasure hunt?"

Aunt Lin's eyes brightened. "Of course."

Me too, Mia almost said, but she bit the words back, embarrassed. Of course she didn't actually remember the Great Treasure Hunt, as Aunt Lin sometimes called it. She hadn't been born yet—her parents had still been little kids, their meeting a faraway glimmer in the future. But Mia lived stories the way other people lived their real lives. So in a way, she remembered.

Something in Ying stirred at this new topic—gave a flush of color to his drabness. His fingers tapped an uneven beat on the tabletop. "I hadn't thought about it in a long time. Not until I heard you were coming back to visit."

"Oh, I still talk about it all the time," Aunt Lin said. "Mia here probably knows everything by heart."

"Does she?" Ying's black brows drew together.

It made the contradictory part of Mia flare up. "Shouldn't I?" she said. She looked to her aunt. "It's *our* treasure."

Aunt Lin laughed. "In a way."

"You told me it was," Mia said stubbornly. "Remember? You said our ancestors knew Zhu Yunwen."

Zhu Yunwen had been a young emperor more than six hundred years ago, during the Ming dynasty in China. He'd ascended the throne as little more than a teenager, but hadn't stayed there long. Less than four years into his rule, his jealous uncle attacked the capital city and drove him away. Then he declared himself emperor, saying that Zhu Yunwen had been killed.

But the only proof the new emperor could produce was a charred body. Legends said that Zhu Yunwen actually escaped his uncle's clutches and fled the capital city disguised as a monk. He then settled into a quiet, anonymous life in the Fujian region of China, but never gave up his hopes of reclaiming his throne—or having his descendants do so for him.

To this end, he hid a great treasure somewhere, hoping to one day fund his return to power. But Zhu Yunwen never saw the perfect opportunity to retake the throne. And over time, the treasure's location faded from memory.

It's still out there, Aunt Lin used to say, curled up beside Mia at bedtime. *Someday, someone will find it.*

They'd lie there whispering in the darkness, dreaming up things the treasure trove might contain: jade bracelets as clear as mountain ice, golden statuettes in the shape of charging horses, piles of jewel-encrusted rings. Mia's voice would grow fainter and fainter until she dozed off and Aunt Lin crept from the room.

Aunt Lin's *In a way* hurt deep in Mia's chest. She sat there on the couch, unsmiling. If it had been Jake beside her, or even her mother, they might not have noticed. But Aunt Lin and Mia were so close that they could sometimes read each other's minds. She noticed.

"Of course I remember," she said, squeezing Mia's hand. "But it's been a very long time since Zhu Yunwen hid that treasure. If anyone found it, it would be an archeological triumph. Something the whole world should share in, and not just us, don't you think?"

"Sure," Mia said, mollified. Like Aunt Lin, she'd never been interested in the treasure's monetary value. Zhu Yunwen's riches were exciting because they were undiscovered, and because they had a wonderful story attached to them. Mia could see no better ending to their journey than the spot of honor in some lovely museum.

Sometimes she dreamed about her and Aunt Lin finding the hoard. Their names would go down in history. That would be better than any number of precious vases or golden coins.

Ying's eyebrows were still bunched up. He stared into his tea.

This had been where he and Aunt Lin had disagreed, all those years ago. He hadn't envisioned Zhu Yunwen's treasure ending up in a museum—he hadn't cared about history, only money. He'd wanted to sell the pieces off one by one, keeping the treasure's location secret while he and Aunt Lin got wealthy.

Neither of us had much money growing up, Aunt Lin had explained to Mia. *You can't blame him for dreaming about a better life.*

Still, the arguments they'd gotten into over it had been bad enough to split up a friendship.

The doorbell sang out. Jake let their mother in, the woman weighed down by shopping bags. Her cheeks were flushed from exertion, but her eyes shined. "Mia, Jake," she said, "you should have come with me. There's so much you haven't seen before—oh, we have a guest?"

Then, of course, introductions had to be made, and snacks brought out, and conversation shifted back to things like travel itineraries and the rising cost of housing. Mia stayed at the table as long as she physically could. Then she caught Jake's eye, and they snuck back to the couch.

The television still blared the same historical drama. A beautiful actress floated across the screen in flowing robes, her head perfectly straight to balance an elaborate headdress. Serving maidens bowed before her, their hands fluttering to one hip.

Mia turned against the couch cushions and nudged at Jake with her toes. "What would you do if you found an emperor's treasure?"

"*Shh*," he said, shoving her foot away. Mia should have known better than to ask Jake something so fantastical, so *unrealistic*. "I'm trying to understand what they're saying."

3

MIA'S STRANGER-UNCLE TRIED TO INSIST THAT
Ying stay for dinner, but the man shook his head and
said he needed to visit his wife at the hospital. Aunt
Lin made him promise he'd return sometime for a
meal and for more remembering. He left her a phone
number and his new address, then slipped away—
very much, Mia thought, the way a shadow leaves a
sunny room.

Aunt Lin didn't seem to share Mia's opinion. She
tucked Ying's address into her notebook with a pleased
little smile and a faraway look.

Mia put this down as an example of strange adult
behavior she didn't understand. Then she put it out of

her mind. There were other things to worry about. Her messenger bag, for example.

She'd lost it somewhere in the apartment earlier that day, and assumed it had fallen beneath Aunt Lin's bed or something. It was a raggedy, beat-up old thing, pieced together from dark green canvas and easily forgotten in dusty corners. Mia's mother had been trying to get rid of it for months.

So Mia's heart jumped when she saw the bag in her stranger-uncle's hand. He and Mia's mother were making up a bed for Jake on the living room couch, and must have found the bag tucked beneath a cushion.

"Is this yours, Jake?" he called before Mia could interrupt him.

Jake poked his head out of the bathroom, his hair still damp from the shower. He laughed. "No, that's Mia's bag of *explorer essentials.*"

Mia flushed. She darted forward and took the messenger bag from her stranger-uncle's grip, hoping against hope that he'd let it go.

He gave her the bag readily enough. But not without saying, amused, "Explorer essentials?"

All three of them were staring at Mia now, of

course—Jake with his stupid grin, their mother with a long-suffering sigh, and Mia's stranger-uncle with his eyebrows raised. If Aunt Lin were there, she might have intervened on Mia's behalf. But she'd insisted on washing the dinner dishes while everyone else prepared for bed.

Grudgingly, Mia met her uncle's gaze. More than anything, she wanted to retreat to Aunt Lin's room without answering. Every time she spoke with her uncle, she felt like she was on the edge of saying something wrong— offending him, maybe. Or just disappointing him.

And this, with her mother and Jake watching, was even worse.

"It's nothing," she managed finally. "It's just a compass my friend gave me . . . and a sewing kit, and matches, and stuff."

Her mother shook her head as she smoothed out the coverlet over the couch, pulling the sheet into perfect lines. "I'm surprised they let her on the plane with those matches. Or the scissors she has in that sewing kit—"

"I told you they would," Mia said. "I looked it up."

"What do you think you're going to need them for?" her stranger-uncle said. He wasn't laughing at her, but his eyes twinkled. Mia had the distinct impression he was making fun of her the way adults sometimes did, like they thought she wouldn't be able to tell.

So she drew herself up and said, with as much dignity as she could, "For emergencies."

The apartment wasn't large, so there weren't enough beds for each of them. Mia had a pallet spread out on the floor of Aunt Lin's room. She didn't mind. It was like a sleepover.

It was hard to believe, though, that six people had once spent their days here—or at least their nights. Aunt Lin said that none of the children had stayed indoors much. The city streets had been their playground from the moment they were old enough to toddle down the five flights of stairs.

Mia had just slipped back into her room to fetch her toothbrush when she saw Aunt Lin hunched over the small desk by the foot of the bed. The room was dark but for her reading light, which lit her in a yellow glow.

"What're you doing?" Mia asked, twirling over on her bare feet. Her towel trailed on the ground behind her.

"Hm?" Aunt Lin was so focused on her notebook, and

on the ponderous movement of her pen, that she hardly seemed to realize Mia was there.

This wasn't unusual when Aunt Lin got interested in something, and Mia just craned her neck to look over Aunt Lin's shoulder. Her aunt had never been a good artist, limited to stick figures and the occasional sketch of a floppy-eared dog. The drawing she worked on now, though shaky, was unmistakably a small, old-fashioned well.

She'd already drawn the hexagonal outer edge and the dark circle in the middle where the bucket descended. Mia watched as she labored over a decorative geometric border etched into the stone.

"Is that Zhu Yunwen's well?" Mia's mouth was right by Aunt Lin's ear, and her voice finally broke the woman from her faraway thoughts. She turned to Mia, blinking. "I thought you didn't remember the pattern on the stone."

"I thought I didn't, either," Aunt Lin said. "But speaking with Ying today jogged my memory."

Together, they studied the drawing of the well. If Aunt Lin's memory was accurate, then this was a replica of the well she'd seen down in the Fujian countryside as a teenager. The very well Zhu Yunwen had drunk from during his harried escape from his murderous uncle. According to local legend, anyway.

He'd been so appreciative of its cool, clear water that years later, after he'd hidden his treasure, he'd left a clue to its location on the well.

Exactly what that clue was, no one knew.

There were many stories about Zhu Yunwen, each a little different. Over the years, Mia had heard them all. Her favorite involved Zhu Yunwen spending the end of his life in a monastery high in the Fujian mountains. On his deathbed, he'd gathered the people closest to him— the few who knew of his real identity—and directed them to hide his treasures someplace safe.

Someplace that could only be found by future generations who understood the clues passed down by his supporters.

Unfortunately, six hundred years is too long for most secrets to be kept alive. The years muddle them into myths, dilute them into hearsay.

Maybe the well did give some indication of Zhu Yunwen's hiding place. Maybe it didn't.

"You don't know how many days and nights Ying and

I studied this thing." Aunt Lin's voice had gone distant again. "There wasn't a lot else to put our minds to out there. Tilling fields and planting rice don't exactly take a lot of mental effort. This was our big mystery. Our puzzle."

Mia leaned against Aunt Lin's shoulder, picking at the woven bracelet around her aunt's wrist. Mia had just made it for her during the plane ride here. "I thought you guys weren't friends anymore. I thought you fought over what you'd do with the treasure if you ever found it."

Aunt Lin laughed. "Oh, we did. We got pretty upset with each other. But that was so long ago. And it was all theoretical in the end. We never figured out Zhu Yuwen's clue." She looked up at Mia. "You don't like him much?"

"I don't know," Mia said, shrugging. She didn't want to talk badly about Aunt Lin's old friend, but there had been something about Ying that made her uneasy. "He doesn't smile. Not ever. He's so serious."

"Well, his wife is very sick," Aunt Lin said. "That's enough to get anyone down, don't you think? Ying told me he was trying to save up money to take her on a trip back to her hometown. It would be very expensive, because she needs a lot of care."

"Couldn't it wait until she got better?" Even as she asked the question, Mia thought she knew the answer.

"Darling, she might not get better again." Aunt Lin kissed Mia on the forehead, her graying curls tickling Mia's cheeks. "Go on and take your shower. Leave an old woman to her memories."

When Mia returned, freshly showered, Aunt Lin was still reminiscing at her desk. She'd pulled out the photo album they'd flipped through earlier that afternoon.

Mia thought about asking her what they might do tomorrow—where they could go first. She hadn't been excited about this trip to China. She'd dragged her feet all the way here, pushing off her packing as long as possible and hoping even as they boarded the plane that something would happen and they'd have to turn back around.

But now that she was here, things were less awful than expected. She missed Thea and Lizbeth and all the things they would have done together this month. But she did have uninterrupted time to hang out with

Aunt Lin. When Mia hung out with Aunt Lin, it always felt like anything could happen—like the line between the imaginary and boring reality got muddled up.

Tomorrow could be the start of an adventure.

Mia curled up amid the blanket-pile beside Aunt Lin's bed and smiled to herself. For years and years, Aunt Lin had shared this exact room with her middle sister. She'd told Mia how they used to tent the blanket above their heads at night, whispering and giggling when they were supposed to be asleep.

It was one thing to hear about a place, though, and another to actually be here.

It made everything that much more real.

Mia closed her eyes, letting herself sink into all the stories Aunt Lin had told her about this apartment. She fell asleep to the soft buzz of the desk lamp.

She woke just once in the middle of the night. Her mind was too sleep-blurred to guess at the time. The desk lamp was still on, but Aunt Lin had moved to sitting cross-legged on the bed, her notebook in her hand. Mia's bleary eyes caught a glimpse of Zhu Yuwen's well.

Aunt Lin's attention was focused on something else—

something laid out in front of her. The blankets blocked it, whatever it was, from Mia's view.

She seems very excited, Mia thought drowsily. Then her eyes slid shut again, and the rest of her thoughts dispersed into dreams.

When she woke the next morning, Aunt Lin's bed was empty. That in itself didn't worry Mia. Her aunt had always been an early riser. Even on weekends, she never got up more than an hour past dawn.

It wasn't until Mia crept into the stillness of the living room, and then the bathroom and the kitchen, that her stomach began to tighten. Everyone else was still asleep. Her mother and stranger-uncle's doors were shut. Jake was sprawled across the couch, his face muffled against his pillow.

"Aunt Lin?" Mia whispered. Then, louder, "Aunt Lin!"

Jake woke with a confused groan. *"Be quiet, Mia."*

But Mia couldn't be quiet.

Aunt Lin was gone.

4

MIA'S MOM WAS THE ONE WHO FOUND THE LETTER
beside the shoe racks.

It had been folded in fourths and was half hidden
in the shadow of Jake's tennis shoes, as if someone had
shoved it just a little too hard beneath the front door.
Mia and Jake crowded on either side of their mom as she
unfolded the piece of paper. Their stranger-uncle was
a heavy sleeper and hadn't woken as they'd tossed the
apartment, looking for signs of Aunt Lin.

Their mom, careful and meticulous in all things, took
her time reading the note.

"What's it say?" Mia said impatiently. Unlike Jake,
Mia could read some Chinese. But she was accustomed

to the perfectly formed, typed characters in her Chinese school textbooks, not the hastily scribbled marks on the note.

"It's from Aunt Lin," Mia's mom said. The words came out like a sigh. "It looks like she got a call from old friends early this morning. They wanted her to come visit, so she set off. She'll be gone a couple of days."

Jake was already turning away. "I knew it."

Mia's mom gave Mia an apologetic smile. "I'm sorry. I know you two had plans."

Mia shook her head. She and Aunt Lin had had more than plans—they'd had a pact. Aunt Lin had promised, and she didn't break her promises. Not to Mia.

"You know how Aunt Lin can be sometimes," her mom said gently. She tried to put a hand on Mia's shoulder, but Mia shied out of the way. She was too upset to be touched.

"She can't be gone." Mia switched back into English, latching on to something familiar and comforting. "She wouldn't leave me here like this."

Something unreadable flashed across her mother's face. Mia snatched up the letter and stared at the words, trying to remember what Aunt Lin's handwriting looked like. She did recognize Aunt Lin's Chinese name at the bottom—*Guo Lin*.

So who else could have written it?

Confusion pushed at Mia's insides like a stormy ocean.

Gently, her mom took the paper from her hands and leaned down so they were eye to eye. Mia had pulled her out of bed to search for Aunt Lin, so she wore nothing but a faded T-shirt and plaid pajama pants, her long hair unbrushed. Even like this, there was something sure and perfect about her.

It should have made Mia feel better, but it didn't.

"I'm sure she'll be back soon, Mia. In the meantime, you and I can still go places, right?"

Her mom didn't understand that that wasn't the point. Aunt Lin was gone. She'd *known* how unhappy Mia was about this trip—how little she'd wanted to come. How much she'd relied on the thought of spending time with Aunt Lin to cheer herself up.

And she was gone anyway.

That meant that either her aunt had abandoned her—or that something else terrible had happened.

She opened her mouth to explain, then shut it again.

She could already tell from the look on her mom's face, and from the sigh in her voice when she'd said *It's from Aunt Lin*, that she didn't doubt Aunt Lin had run off again.

Nothing Mia said would convince her otherwise. Especially if the only proof Mia had was the fact that Aunt Lin had made her a promise. She'd think Mia was being silly. Even if she didn't *say* that, Mia would be able to see it in her eyes.

Sometimes, her mother was *too* sure about things.

"Here," her mom said, reaching for her purse. She took out a few coins and pressed them into Mia's hand. "You and Jake need to get out of the apartment a little. Why don't you go see what the street venders are selling for breakfast?"

Despite the early hour, the sun was already out in full force. Mia scuffed her shoes as she and Jake wandered beyond the apartment complex's tall, metal gate. In the town outside Memphis, Tennessee, where she usually lived, the sidewalks and roads would be all but abandoned at this hour. Here in Fuzhou, the streets weren't exactly clogged, but they weren't empty, either.

A woman strolled ahead of them with a waddling

corgi puppy. A businessman hurried past, running for the nearby bus stop. Jake pulled Mia out of the way as an old man rode by on a bicycle, pulling a rickety cart piled high with leafy vegetables. The wheels splashed dirty water from the gutters. Everyone seemed lost in their very separate lives, no one paying the least attention to Mia and Jake.

That, too, was different. Back home, people nodded and smiled at each other on the streets. But Mia supposed that was easier to do when their town was so little, they barely had streetlights.

The sidewalks got even busier as they rounded the corner. Here, venders lined the sides of the roads, peddling everything from stacks of steamed buns to basins of gasping fish. Some had tiny storefronts. Others only had carts. Boiling oil gurgled away in enormous pots or sizzled in pans as cooks fried up ever-growing piles of scallion pancakes.

Choosing breakfast here was certainly more exciting than it was at home, where Mia climbed onto the counters to reach for cold cereal.

Still, Mia felt Aunt Lin's absence like an icy ghost at her side. If her aunt had been here, she would have taken Mia to all the venders, suggested things for her to try, and told her stories about cooking for her siblings when she was younger. She would have laughed and chatted with the cooks, sweeping Mia up in the cheer of her personality.

"What do you want to eat?" Jake said.

Mia shrugged and fiddled with the strap of her messenger bag.

To her surprise, Jake didn't get annoyed with her nonanswer, the way he usually did nowadays. Instead, he pulled her to one of the venders selling *you tiao*.

Mia had eaten *you tiao* before in America, but they'd come frozen from the Chinese market. These were hot out of the wok. She watched as the street vender plopped strips of dough into the bubbling oil, where they turned golden as they puffed up. A quick flip over, and they were done. Jake bought them one each.

Mia knew she ought to wait for them to cool down a little, but she managed to be patient only a few seconds. The *you tiao* was perfect: crispy on the outside, fluffy within.

They picked up milk next, which didn't come in bottles or cartons here, but in little plastic bags. Mia ripped a hole in the corner to drink. It tasted different, too, though she couldn't put her finger on how.

The food bolstered her spirits. The early morning hustle and bustle seemed more friendly and less intimidating. It gave her a clearer view on Aunt Lin's disappearance, too.

There was simply no way her aunt had abandoned her like this.

She thought back to the last time she'd seen her aunt, right before she'd fallen asleep. No, that wasn't right. She'd seen her after that. She'd woken up in the middle of the night and seen . . .

What had she seen?

Aunt Lin had been sitting cross-legged on the bed. She'd been studying something. The drawing of Zhu Yunwen's well.

Maybe her disappearance had something to do with the emperor's lost treasure.

"What is it, Mia?" Jake said.

Mia blinked. She hadn't realized she'd frozen right in the middle of the sidewalk.

Jake frowned at her. It still disoriented Mia sometimes, how tall he was now. It was like gremlins had crept in one night and stolen her brother away—her old brother, who didn't mind cartoons and liked chopstick sword fights—replacing him with a gangly-armed skyscraper who slathered gel in his hair. Who spent half his days looking at Mia like he couldn't believe they were related.

"Look," Jake said, "you can't get too upset about Aunt Lin leaving, okay? It's like Mom said. She'll be back soon, and in the meantime, you can do stuff without her. You don't have to be attached at the hip all the time."

"We're not," Mia said.

I just have a feeling that something is wrong, she wanted to say but didn't know if she should. If Jake would just roll his eyes and say she was blowing things out of proportion or letting her imagination run away with her.

Before she could make up her mind, Jake had already turned away again, heading farther down the street.

Mia ran to keep up.

5

BACK AT THE APARTMENT, MIA MADE A BEELINE
for the bedroom she shared with Aunt Lin. She hadn't
thought to check Aunt Lin's bed closely this morning—
she'd seen that her aunt wasn't in it, and that had been
enough. Now, she flipped through the rumpled blanket until
her fingers closed around Aunt Lin's discarded notebook.

They brushed against something else, too. Frowning,
Mia pulled a picture frame from beneath the spiral-bound
notebook. It was the painting of the two cranes. The one
Mia's grandmother had loved and hidden away during the
Chinese Cultural Revolution.

They'd put it back in the trunk before Ying arrived.
Had Aunt Lin retrieved it last night?

Mia shifted the painting into her lap—and startled as the painting slid from the frame. Someone—Aunt Lin?—had popped the two apart. Gingerly, she slipped the painting the rest of the way free. Traditional Chinese brush paintings were done on rice paper, as thin and fragile as butterfly wings. This one had been mounted onto a sheet of heavier board, but it still felt tenuous in Mia's hands, as if one careless motion might tear it down the middle.

The dancing cranes shimmered in the morning light. Mia tilted them this way and that, her eyes roaming across the rolling landscape behind them. She'd forgotten to ask Aunt Lin how old this painting was—or how it had come into their family.

Despite all of Aunt Lin's stories, there were so many things Mia didn't know about her relatives here in China. She could recite more about a six-hundred-year-old emperor than she could about her own grandparents.

Was that why Aunt Lin had gotten the painting out of storage again? Had she wanted to remember Mia's grandmother, or tell Mia something?

It was impossible to say.

Mia sighed and flipped the painting over, preparing to pop it back into the frame. She was so focused on being careful, on making sure nothing got crinkled or bent, that it took her several seconds to realize what she was seeing.

There was something sketched on the back.

It was hand-drawn, spindly black lines stretching across the stiff paper in geometric patterns. It looked like a more chaotic version of a window lattice, or an imprint of a fancy balustrade design, the marks looping into half-moons or zigzagging in neat corners. At five different places, they disappeared entirely, leaving big blank spaces in the—

In the what? What was this?

Mia's heart thumped against her ribs.

She didn't dare move—barely dared to blink, as if that might make the mysterious lines disappear.

Everything was faded with age, but Mia made out columns of neat calligraphy beside each blank spot. Most of the characters were unfamiliar. They looked like traditional, complex Chinese, which Mia had never learned. Almost everyone in China learned the simplified versions of characters nowadays.

If Aunt Lin were here, Mia could seek her help. But she wasn't. Did her disappearance have something to do with this strange drawing? She must have found it last night. Maybe that was why she'd looked so excited.

Then what? What had happened afterward?

Mia flipped through Aunt Lin's notebook, hoping for answers. On the last page was the sketch of Zhu Yunwen's well. Her aunt had made a small addition to the drawing— she'd circled part of the well's repeating geometric pattern. Beside it, in her hurried handwriting, she'd scribbled: *Clue #5.*

"Clue five," Mia muttered, turning back to the drawing. She studied each of the blank portions, trying to work her way through the characters written beside each one. None of them were numbered, so Aunt Lin must have come up with her own system.

It was no good. She couldn't read enough of the characters to make sense of anything.

"What're you doing?"

Mia nearly fell off the bed in surprise. Jake stood in the doorway, one hand propped against the doorjamb. Before she could cobble together an answer, he crossed to the bed and tugged the painting out of her hands, ignoring her protest.

"What's this?" He raised his eyebrow at her. "Where did you find this?"

"It was Grandma's favorite painting," Mia said. She felt a little defensive, though she wasn't sure why. "Aunt Lin showed it to me yesterday. It was on her bed."

Jake frowned at the black lines, then flipped the canvas over and looked at the cranes on the other side—before turning back to the patterns again. "This must be ancient. What does the writing say?"

It usually made Mia feel rather proud—and maybe just a little superior—when Jake asked her to translate some Chinese. But right now, she had to admit that she couldn't read enough to know.

Jake took out his phone. In a moment, he'd pulled up a Chinese dictionary application. He handed it to Mia, a glint of something like cautious excitement in his eyes.

It took them a while to translate even one collection of characters. But by the time they were halfway through, Mia could guess what it was—a description of a place.

A *clue*.

She read her rough translation aloud when they were done:

> *At the foot of the mountains*
> *Sweet water flows, singing*
> *Not only in the rivers*
> *But pulled from the earth.*
> *Seek me at the edge of the ring.*

"A well," Mia said. "That's what it's talking about—a well."

She looked at Jake, and Jake looked at her.

They spoke together: "Zhu Yunwen's well—"

Mia rushed to look at Aunt Lin's drawing again, and at the pattern she'd circled. What had she meant?

Then it clicked. She grabbed the pencil and copied the pattern from the well onto the blank portion of the lines—the one beside what Aunt Lin must have designated *Clue #5*. It fit perfectly, matching up with the design already present.

Then she sat back and looked up at Jake, wide-eyed.

Treasure map, cried Mia's thoughts. What else could it be?

A lot of things, whispered the more practical part of her. The part that spoke in her mother's calm voice and rolled its eyes just like Jake.

But Jake wasn't rolling his eyes right now. He looked just as stunned as she felt.

If Mia's intuition was right, this wasn't just any map.

It wasn't even just any treasure map.

It was *Zhu Yunwen's* treasure map, and if they managed to solve every clue—fill in every blank space—they could have a map leading right to his long-lost hoard.

6

MIA'S MIND REELED.

Hadn't Aunt Lin always said that their ancestors had known Zhu Yunwen? Been his friends and secret supporters? If the emperor *had* left a map, it made sense that it might end up in Mia's family, passed down generation after generation until everyone forgot the heirloom's significance.

Had Aunt Lin realized all this last night? She must have been as excited as Mia felt now—like she was tilting on the edge of something wonderful, and vast, and thrilling.

Then she'd gotten a call from a friend in the morning and left?

No. That story made even less sense now.

Mia's brow scrunched up in thought. Why would Aunt Lin leave the house? Why hadn't she immediately woken Mia to share the good news?

She flipped through the rest of Aunt Lin's notebook. It wasn't big—Mia had bought it for her aunt during the last school book fair, and she'd chosen it more for the unique, pale blue pages than for actual utility. Inside, there wasn't much of interest—a packing list for their trip, a jotted flight itinerary, a few telephone numbers Aunt Lin had wanted in hand while they were overseas. And one page, ripped out. Mia ran her fingers over the ragged blue edge left behind.

Then she squinted at the blank page beneath it. She tilted the notebook up, toward the window, and stared at the divots that had been carved into the page—a ghostly impression of the missing page that had lain on top of it. Aunt Lin always pressed too hard when she wrote.

But this wasn't writing. These lines were remnants of a drawing.

A copy of the map.

Mia tilted the notebook a little more, and a slip of

paper fell out, stark white against the dark red blanket.

An address was scribbled on it.

Ying's address.

There was only one person Aunt Lin might have wanted to tell before Mia. The person who'd started this search with her so many years ago.

Mia hesitated. Jake had seemed excited about the treasure map, but that was different—that was something tangible he could hold in his hands. This suspicion niggling at the back of Mia's mind was something else entirely. Something he might laugh at.

"If Aunt Lin figured all this out last night," Mia said carefully, "she might have wanted to share it with Ying. Since they worked on the treasure hunt together before."

She waited, breath held, for Jake's reply.

He gave her a long look. "You don't think Aunt Lin just went to visit a friend."

Mia shook her head.

"Well, if she and Ying are really out there chasing down clues," he said, cracking a smile, "I guess that's not terrible. Aunt Lin could be famous by the end of this trip."

Mia couldn't think about Ying without thinking about

the unsmiling way he'd looked at her all afternoon. The way his eyebrows had knit after Aunt Lin revealed that she'd told Mia all about Zhu Yunwen's treasure.

Maybe Aunt Lin was right, and Ying was just dour because he was worried about his wife. Maybe he was a nice person, despite how he'd seemed.

But either way, he might know where Aunt Lin had gone.

"I have to know for sure where she is," Mia said. "I have—I have to go talk to him, Jake."

Jake tapped his finger against the side of the picture frame. He looked from the translated clue to the blank portions of the map, then back again.

"All right," he said. "Let's finish translating these riddles. Then we'll visit Ying."

Mia's mother and stranger-uncle were just finishing up breakfast, the former scrolling through e-mails on her laptop while the latter read the morning paper. Both were still in their pajamas.

Jake and Mia shot each other a look before stepping into the dining area. There was always a game plan to asking their mother for something. By this point, they knew all of the moves instinctually, but it was good to touch base beforehand, even if only through a glance.

Jake went first, pulling up a chair and saying, "Mia and I were thinking about going to see Ying today. You know, because his wife is sick. We could bring him something."

Their mom gave him a surprised smile. "That's sweet of you. But shouldn't you wait until Aunt Lin gets back? Then you could go with her. She knows Ying best, after all."

That was Mia's cue to wander closer to the table. "We don't know when Aunt Lin's getting back." It wasn't hard to make sure she looked upset.

"Mia—" their mom said. It sounded like the placating start of a sentence that would end with *no*, and Jake quickly interrupted: "I wanted to go check out that big supermarket Uncle was talking about. We could pick up something there."

Their stranger-uncle had spent the whole conversation peering at them over the top of his paper. Now he grinned. It was weird to see a man lounging around the breakfast table beside Mia's mother—even if it was her own brother. Usually, only Mia, Jake, and Aunt Lin were privy to her early morning rumpled hair and unlined eyes.

But here she sat next to Mia's uncle, as casual as if she did it every day.

"I have plans to meet up with some old classmates for lunch," she said. "If you two can wait until afterward, I'll go with you—"

"I think we can get around by ourselves, Mom." Jake looped his arm around Mia's shoulder. "Mia can read the street signs, right?"

Mia nodded vigorously. "Right."

She felt their mother wavering. Back home, she let Mia and Jake run free around town. Between her own long hours at work and Aunt Lin's sometimes unpredictable shifts at a local shop, there wasn't always someone home to keep tabs on them anyway. But home was home.

There was a whole other country outside these apartment doors, and Mia figured her mother might need an extra push toward *yes*.

Please, she begged her with her eyes. Aloud, she just said, "What else are we supposed to do while you're out for lunch? We'll just be stuck here."

Ten minutes later, they were yanking on their shoes and scrambling out the door. Mia barely heard their mother as she called out after them: "Be careful! Come straight back afterward! And make sure you stick together!"

It was even hotter now, the city furnacelike in the summer heat. Some of the young women on the streets carried parasols to shade their faces, but Mia and Jake made do without, squinting at the road signs as they hurried past.

Ying's apartment wasn't far at all. They made a quick stop at the supermarket to pick up a fancy-looking tin of cookies, then hurried across a small bridge, headed for the address Ying had left behind. Mia was so focused on finding their way that when they came upon the high-rise, she felt slightly disoriented.

She fell behind, letting Jake take the lead. Part of her demanded more time to prepare. Though to prepare for what, she wasn't sure.

They caught an elderly lady on her way inside the building. She smiled and held the door open for them. All three of them squeezed into the tiny elevator, Mia clutching the tin of cookies to her chest.

How are you? she rehearsed in her head, picturing

Ying's solemn face. *We brought you something for your wife. We hope she's doing well.*

Then what?

The elevator lurched upward. Mia's stomach seemed to get left behind, making her queasy. Or maybe it was just the questions swirling around in her mind: *By the way, did you know Aunt Lin went missing?*

Did she come visit you last night?

Did she tell you about the treasure map?

Do you know where she is now?

There were only two apartments on Ying's floor, one directly to the left of the elevator, the other to the right. Jake and Mia tried to leave just as the elderly lady stepped forward to do the same; they bumped together in an awkward jumble. The old woman laughed and waved her hands when Jake apologized.

"Are you looking for Ying?" she asked, gesturing to the left-side door. "I'm his neighbor."

The lady's door was cheerily decorated with a diamond of red paper. On it, written upside down in gold, was the character for "good fortune." The Chinese word for "upside down" was a homonym with the word for "arrive," so decorations like these were common. They were supposed to bring happiness to the homes within.

Ying's door was bare. Perhaps he wasn't the superstitious sort. Or perhaps, Mia thought glumly, he was too surly for something so bright and cheery.

"Our aunt is an old friend of his," Jake said. "We heard his wife was ill and wanted to bring something."

The old lady raised her eyebrows. "Didn't he tell you he'd be away?"

Mia's fingers tightened around the cookie tin. The queasy feeling in her stomach churned harder. "No, he didn't."

"Maybe I'm mistaken," the woman said. "I thought I saw him in the parking lot last night, loading a suitcase into his van. But it was dark, and my eyesight isn't what it used to be. . . ."

Jake had the presence of mind to thank her as she disappeared into her apartment. Mia could only force herself to press Ying's doorbell.

They stood in the tiny hallway and waited. And waited.

And waited some more.

Mia jabbed the doorbell again.

"Guess he really isn't home," Jake said.

Half desperate, Mia reached out to ring the doorbell a third time. Then her eyes caught something lying on the ground. It was shoved up against the bottom edge of the door, crumpled into a ball, but as soon as Mia saw it, she knew what it was: Aunt Lin's woven bracelet.

The very one Mia had made for her during the plane ride to China.

There was no doubt about it. Aunt Lin had been here.

And now both she and Ying were gone.

7

"IT DOESN'T NECESSARILY MEAN ANYTHING, Mia," Jake said as they walked back home. He carried the cookie tin now, because Mia only had eyes for Aunt Lin's bracelet. "Are you even sure it's—"

"It's hers. I *made* it. I know what it looks like. And look, it didn't just slip off. Someone cut it, right here."

Jake gamely looked where she was pointing.

"I think it's a signal," Mia said. "I think it's Aunt Lin telling us something went wrong."

Both she and Jake had switched to speaking in English. If any of the people walking past understood them, no one showed it. Back home, Mia and Aunt Lin often used Chinese to talk about secret things in public places. Using English in China seemed to work just as well.

"What do you mean, 'went wrong'?" Jake said.

"I don't know—what if he took her?"

"As in *kidnapped* her? You're just saying that because you didn't like him, Mia. What would he do that for?"

Mia's reply burst from her like a thunderclap. "Because she told him about the map! Because he realized that if he let Aunt Lin come home, she'd tell everyone in the morning. And if everyone knew, then it wouldn't be a secret and he couldn't go find Zhu Yunwen's treasure for himself. He couldn't just keep it and sell it the way he's always wanted to!"

Now people did turn and stare. Jake hustled Mia into an alley behind a hole-in-the-wall restaurant. The trash bins here reeked of fish guts and rotting vegetables, but they had their privacy.

He crossed his arms. "You can't just say things like that, Mia. You can't accuse people of being kidnappers—not without good reason."

I have a good reason, Mia thought. *I have lots of good reasons.*

But she stayed quiet, her jaw set, her hand fisted around Aunt Lin's severed bracelet. If Jake didn't believe her, then their mom probably wouldn't either. And then what could Mia do? How could she help Aunt Lin?

"You're always being like this." Jake sighed. "You hate new people. You don't like Ying. You don't like our uncle—"

"Those are two completely different things. And I never said I didn't like our uncle. I just—" Mia didn't know how to express her feelings out loud. Didn't know how to put the tangle in her chest into words. Especially not words someone like Jake would understand. She faltered, struggling.

Jake didn't wait for her to try again.

"Besides," he said, "even *if* everything else you're saying really did happen, Ying wouldn't have the map. It's still at home on Aunt Lin's bed, remember?"

He looked at her as if that were enough to explain everything. To make everything okay.

"She made a copy," Mia said. "The ripped-out page— she must have drawn the map on it. She wouldn't have wanted to take the painting out on the streets. Not once she realized how old it was. She would've copied down the map to show Ying."

Jake sighed, as if Mia were talking gibberish. She

started to tell him about the imprint of Aunt Lin's pen—how that was proof of everything. But his sigh strangled the rest of her words.

If Mia was right, then Ying would be rushing to complete the treasure map right now. If Mia got to the treasure first, then she'd have what he wanted. And he'd have what she wanted: Aunt Lin. A trade might be made. Mia would give up any treasure in the world if it meant Aunt Lin's safe return.

If Mia was mistaken, then Aunt Lin was visiting friends, like her letter said, and nothing was wrong at all.

If Mia was mistaken, then this would just end up another time when her imagination had run away with her. Another instance of her being *impetuous* and *childish*.

Cotton-candy-headed. Weird.

Maybe Jake was right and all the clues were just coincidences.

But what if they weren't?

Mia couldn't just go back to the apartment and forget about everything—not if there was the smallest possibility that Aunt Lin was in danger.

She thought back to the riddle they'd translated. The answer had seemed obvious, but that was only because she'd grown up hearing about Zhu Yunwen's well. Could she solve the other riddles as easily?

Even if she did, what if the locations they described were as far away as the well? Her mother would never let her go by herself.

Mia hesitated, her fingers twisting around Aunt Lin's bracelet. She squeezed it in her fist. No matter what, she had to try.

"The treasure map's real," she said, and waited until Jake gave a grudging nod. "That means Zhu Yunwen's treasure is—*could be* real. We could still figure out the riddles together. If you wanted."

It was much more likely that their mom would let Mia leave the apartment if Jake was with her. Besides, a part of Mia didn't want to do this alone. Jake could irritate her to no end, and get in the way, and half the time he barely took her seriously. But the unfamiliar streets felt less daunting when he was around. Even if Mia was the one who could read the road signs.

She felt him hesitate. Felt him get ready to tell her that this was a wild-goose chase.

"All right," Jake said instead.

Maybe he was only agreeing because he had nothing

better to do in this faraway country—but right now that was good enough.

Hope sparked in Mia's chest. "You won't tell Mom?"

If their mom found out about the map, she'd confiscate it. She wasn't the sort to believe in searching for lost treasure. She probably wouldn't even believe the map was real until it got authenticated by an expert—just like she wouldn't believe that Aunt Lin had been kidnapped until Mia had better proof of that, too.

"I won't tell Mom." Jake stuck out his hand, and they shook on it.

When they'd been younger, they'd sealed hundreds of promises this way: oaths to stick together at summer camp, or to back each other up in an argument, or to not eat the last of the ice cream while the other was away at soccer practice.

Back then it had felt like something unbreakable. Like the heavens might open up and strike them dead if they went back on their promise. It felt less like that now. But Mia still trusted in the promises Jake made her.

A cook, his white apron stained with splashes of oil and sauces, pushed out of the back door into the alley.

He startled at the sight of Mia and Jake, his hands pausing midway toward lighting his cigarette.

"What're you doing here?" he said, annoyed. "This is no place for you kids to play around."

Jake grabbed Mia's hand, and they hurried back onto the main street.

Mia's stranger-uncle was the first to see them when they arrived back home. As usual, he gave Mia a big smile, and as usual, she barely managed one in return.

"You still have the cookies—wasn't he home?" he said, and Mia stayed quiet, so Jake had to answer.

Afterward, when they were safe in the privacy of Aunt Lin's bedroom, Jake said, "You should talk to him, you know. Say 'good morning' and stuff, at least."

He sounded just like their mom sometimes.

Mia grabbed the notebook with their translated riddles, and pushed the painting toward Jake, along with a pencil. "If we're going to do this, we should trace out a copy of the map so we can carry it around."

She looked through the four unsolved riddles while he drew the map. None of them seemed to have an obvious answer. But then, maybe that was just because she didn't know the area. If the riddles had described places around her little hometown—the water park where she and her best friends spent each summer, the horse ranch where Thea's mother worked, the strip mall where everyone hung out after school—Mia would have been able to guess them, no problem.

But Fuzhou was a big city, and Fujian was a huge province. And what if the clues were meant to direct them even farther? To other provinces in China?

She took a deep breath and read the first riddle aloud. Maybe Jake would see some sense in it. "'Jutting above the world on nine glazed layers, one thousand buddha chant in unison. Their voices are backed by the peal of heavenly bells. Below frolic a ring of roaring lions—find me in the ring above their cages.'"

Jake looked up from his drawing. "Lions? Either these are images of lions, or it's talking about a zoo."

"Did they have zoos back then?" Mia said. Even if they had, it wasn't like they could expect the zoo to still exist. "Zhu Yunwen must have known that it might be a long time before his treasure was found. He would've chosen things that were more permanent than a zoo."

Still, there was *a long time*, and then there was *more than half a millennium*.

For a moment, Mia felt so daunted by her task that she faltered.

She took a deep breath. Things were just beginning— she couldn't be scared already. Besides, Aunt Lin might be counting on her.

Just think of it as an adventure, she told herself. *Think of it as a story.*

One, she hoped, with a happy ending.

8

MIA PONDERED THE RIDDLE THE REST OF THE
morning, her thoughts jumping from possibility to
possibility.

> *Jutting above the world on nine glazed layers*
> *One thousand buddha chant in unison.*
> *Their voices are backed by the peal of heavenly bells.*

Maybe the riddle was talking about a temple or a
monastery. But what did the bit about the "nine glazed
layers" mean? And what about the "ring of roaring lions"?
Lion statues were common around China, but usually
there was just a pair of them outside an entryway. She

couldn't remember ever seeing a whole ring of them. And they were never sculpted in cages.

"What do you think, Mia?"

Mia blinked and realized that everyone at the table was staring at her. Jake and their stranger-uncle were partway through a game of cards. Mia's mother put on a pair of earrings as she readied to leave for her lunch.

Her stranger-uncle laughed. "I said, the Fuzhou National Park is pretty this time of year. It's a little farther away, but it might be nice to get out of the city and take a look, don't you think?"

Mia ducked her head. "Yeah, I guess so."

There was a pause, as if everyone was waiting for her to say more. Only there wasn't more Mia wanted to say.

An eon later, the conversation turned to something else. Mia's mom shot her a look across the table. It was only the tiniest raise of her perfect eyebrows, the smallest quirk of her mouth, but Mia knew what it meant: *Please be polite, Mia.*

Please make nice conversation, and smile, and don't just get lost in your own world.

But that was one kind of pretending Mia wasn't good at. Jake was. He kept the conversation going about basketball, and soccer, and where was the next World Cup going to be, again?

Mia slipped from the table, stopping by her mother's bedroom to turn on the wireless router before retreating to Aunt Lin's room. Her uncle wasn't very computer savvy, so he only paid for a limited number of hours of Internet access a day—something Mia had never heard about before. Her mom had warned Jake that he couldn't spend all day playing games online the way he sometimes did at home. Not only was the wireless too slow for that, but they didn't want to make their uncle pay overage fees.

Mia figured if anything was worth using the Internet for, it was researching to solve Zhu Yunwen's riddles.

She started by searching temples in the area. The first result that came up was someplace called Xichan Temple. One tourist review site called it "beautiful and peaceful." Another blogger showed pictures of green ponds and little turtles sunbathing on logs.

Hualin Temple, the next one she clicked on, was apparently the oldest wooden structure in all of South China and now served as a museum. Interesting, but the riddle hadn't mentioned wood.

Ten minutes later, Mia realized there were a whole lot of temples within Fuzhou's city limits alone. There were even more beyond them. And none of the links she explored said anything about chanting buddhas, or heavenly bells, or lions frolicking in cages.

A knock came at the door.

"Mia?" her mom said.

"Come in," she replied distractedly, and only looked up when a small pile of brochures landed beside her on the bed.

"Oh, good," her mom said, sounding pleased. "You're looking up places to visit. I didn't know you were interested in temples."

She'd changed into a sleek black skirt and light blue blouse, her hair falling in a perfectly straight sheet around her shoulders. The diamonds in her ears twinkled. Beside her, lounging in a pair of scruffy jeans and a tank top, Mia felt like the two of them lived in different dimensions. Their worlds touched, but just barely.

Her mother patted her on the shoulder. "Let me know where you want to go, okay? Here are some tourist pamphlets your uncle gathered before we arrived. They're in English, so show them to Jake, too."

"Mmm," Mia said, throwing the brochures a cursory glance. She hoped her mom wouldn't probe more about her sudden interest in Buddhist temples.

Luckily, she didn't. Unluckily, she said instead, "Your uncle is really excited to get to know you guys, you know. And he's done a lot to make you feel at home."

Mia kept her eyes on the computer screen. Her mom's words made her uncomfortably guilty. And if anything, that guilt just made her want to avoid her uncle even more. He didn't *need* to be that nice to her. She'd be perfectly happy to have them both pretend the other didn't exist.

Her mom sighed when Mia didn't reply. "Maybe just start with thanking him for the brochures?"

Mia's shoulders hunched. "Okay."

"Okay," her mom said, and bent to kiss Mia on the temple. She smelled faintly like roses. "I'm off. Don't spend too long on the computer."

It was another fifteen minutes before Mia turned from the laptop, frustrated and no closer to a breakthrough. She threw herself against the pillows and stared at the ceiling, her arms splayed out on either side of her.

"Where are you?" she whispered to Aunt Lin, or the ceiling, or maybe both.

Neither gave her a reply.

She rolled onto her side, her gaze falling on the glossy brochures. The one on top was for the Fuzhou National Park. There were strange, stringy-looking trees in the background, surrounded by blue skies and puffy white clouds.

It *was* nice of her stranger-uncle to collect these for them. Sighing, she grabbed the bundle and sat up again. Her hands fisted in the blanket. Maybe time away from the riddle would help. Wasn't Aunt Lin always saying that?

Just take a break, she'd tell Mia. *Think about something else for a while. You'll be surprised what your brain does when you don't think it's paying attention.*

Of course, Aunt Lin was the only person in Mia's life who ever encouraged her to pay *less* attention to things. With everyone else, it was always, *Focus, Mia. Stop getting distracted, Mia. Why can't you just concentrate harder?*

But Aunt Lin was a daydreamer too.

As a child, her favorite place to dream or to ponder her problems had been here, in this apartment.

Mia straightened.

Well, not exactly *in* the apartment.

Mia took a deep breath as she padded onto the apartment's balcony. The sunbaked boards warmed her feet. The balcony wasn't big—Mia could have leaped from one side to the other without much trouble. It was made even smaller by a family of potted plants and the string of laundry hanging overhead. But an awning blocked the worst of the summer sun, and the smallness was kind of cozy.

Mia sat beside the balustrade and tilted her face downward, staring at the street below. Had things looked the same down there when Aunt Lin was a child? If only Aunt Lin were here and they could talk about it.

Still, just this—sitting here where her aunt had sat once upon a time—was nice. Back home, Thea sometimes took Mia around her family's horse barn and said things like, *My grandpa built that shed over there with my dad and my uncles, a long time ago,* or *My great-grandma made this quilt. My mom says I'll get to have it one day, when I'm older.*

Mia had never really had things like that. Only stories.

She'd never thought she'd missed having things like that either. Not until this moment, with her fingers curled around the balcony railing and a thrumming, singing feeling rushing through her veins. A feeling that, like many of Mia's feelings, couldn't easily fit into words.

Maybe it was something like: *I came from this.*

Something like: *I'm a part of this.*

Something like: *I belong.*

Mia smiled. Calmer now, she turned back to the brochures and shuffled through them. Beneath the one for Fuzhou National Park lay a pamphlet with a tower on the front. Each level's roof winged out like the fancy roofs of a pagoda, bells hanging from their eaves. Above them, little men stood with their hands clasped in front of them.

No, not little men—little buddhas.

Jutting above the world on nine glazed layers,
One thousand buddha chant in unison.
Their voices are backed by the peal of heavenly bells.

Mia sat up ramrod straight. "Thousand Buddha Pottery Pagoda," she read off the bottom of the pamphlet.

She rushed through the rest of the pages, searching for a wider view of the pagoda, and found one on the very last page.

She counted the levels of the tower: *one, two, three, four, five, six, seven, eight, nine.*

"Jake!" she shouted.

9

JAKE WAS HUNCHED IN A CORNER OF THEIR
mother's room, video-chatting with a friend back home.
He mouthed at Mia to leave him alone and shut the door
behind her. She was too excited to be upset.

Her stranger-uncle had the TV tuned to a news
channel, but he put it on mute when he saw Mia edging
up to him with the brochure in hand.

All her words came rushing out at once: "Can Jake and
I go here? To the Yongquan Temple? It's not that far. I
figured out how we could get there by bus. We have the
money. We go around by ourselves all the time at home."

"Wait, slow down," he said, laughing. He reached for
the brochure. "Which temple?"

"Yongquan," Mia said. "I want to see the Thousand Buddha Pottery Pagoda."

"Right now? With your mother away?"

It made sense to wait for her mom to come home. But there was no way she'd be back in time to go today. They'd have to wait until tomorrow at the earliest. The very thought made Mia's chest tighten. She was already filled with the jittery need to leave—was already itching to be gone *now*, if not five minutes ago.

"What's the rush?" her stranger-uncle said. "So bored already?"

Mia hesitated. "I don't like to be cooped up."

He leaned forward, his elbows on his knees. "I didn't either, when I was your age. My friends and I were out on the streets from the time school let out until it was time for dinner. And afterward, if there was any light left—out we'd go again."

His friendly chattiness reminded Mia of Aunt Lin. Mia's mom wasn't the sort to go on unnecessarily or to talk just to fill a silence.

"So," she said hopefully, "can Jake and I go?"

He winked at her. "If you can be back before your mother gets home."

Mia barged back into her mother's room, brushing aside Jake's irritated *"Go away, Mia—come on."*

"I solved the first clue," she hissed at him. "We have to leave now if we're going to make it back in time."

"In time for what?" he said, but she'd darted out the door again, going to grab her messenger bag and the copy of Zhu Yunwen's map. She paused, just for a few seconds, in the living room.

It took a moment for her tongue to get around the words, but she faced her stranger-uncle and said, a little shyly, "Thanks. For the brochures."

She even managed a smile.

At the bus stop, Jake hovering over her shoulder, Mia watched carefully to see what the other people did as they boarded. Most swiped cards over a bar code reader by the driver's seat. Others dropped coins into a slot.

When their bus came, Mia fed in the fee for two tickets and tried to look like she'd been doing this all her life.

There weren't any empty seats, so she and Jake found a spot to stand toward the back. Jake was tall enough to reach the handrail, but Mia had to clutch the back of a seat as the bus lurched along.

The streets of Fuzhou thronged with cars and bicycles and people on brightly colored mopeds. Everyone zoomed and shoved from one lane to another like tangled strands in a tapestry.

"What a road hazard," Lizbeth's father always said when someone cut in front of his car, or slammed on their brakes, or didn't stop properly at a pedestrian walk. He was very fond of what he called the Rules of the Road.

Mia was pretty sure he'd think all the drivers in China were road hazards. If there were Rules of the Road here, they were a lot looser than they were back home. But they reached their destination—a shopping complex where they needed to change buses—safe and sound. By then, Mia was too occupied with thoughts of the Thousand Buddha Pottery Pagoda to think about much else.

Outside the bus window, the city streets changed to winding, tree-lined roads. Yongquan Temple was halfway up a mountain, and soon, said mountain rose before them, softly green against the blue sky. The bus carried them beneath a looming gate with Chinese-style roofs and a pair of lions guarding either side.

Then, finally, it pulled up to the sidewalk. Mia and Jake tumbled out along with a sizable group of fellow tourists. Most were Chinese, but there was a couple that seemed to be visiting from Japan, and a young Englishwoman who continued chatting on her phone as the bus rumbled off again in a cloud of exhaust.

Schools let out later in China for summer vacation, so there weren't other kids around who were Mia's and Jake's ages. But little kids ran about playing tag or held on to their caretaker's hands. Mia watched as an old lady handed a little girl—her granddaughter, maybe?—an ice-cream bar from the nearby snack stands. The scene was both familiar and unfamiliar, like a well-loved picture cast in different colors.

"Come on," Jake said, pulling Mia deeper into the park. "I thought you were in a hurry."

According to the pamphlet Mia still carried in her bag, there were three different routes they could take up to the Yongquan Temple. Vans loitered around the parking lot, their drivers calling out to passersby, offering to drive up them up the mountain for a fee.

"There's a cable car, too," said the snack vender when Mia asked for directions. She grinned at them. "But walking is better. You can see sights on the way up."

Of course, Mia couldn't leave without buying something from her ice-cream cart—just to be polite. She bit into the ice pop as they started up the path, taking the first flight of what seemed to be a great number of stone-cut stairs. A breeze rustled the leaves, making their shadows dance.

The main road split often, each meandering path marked by a wooden sign. They advertised beautiful waterfalls, scenic rock formations, or vantage points for ancient inscriptions carved into stone. Mia and Jake wandered past a few of the etched characters, their heads craned back to see the ones higher up.

Some were huge and bright red against the gray rocks. Others were smaller, more subtle. Snippets of a tour guide's practiced patter floated by as he led a large group of tourists, hoisting a bright yellow flag to show the way. Apparently, some of these inscriptions dated from the Song dynasty—one thousand years ago.

I'm so jealous, Thea had said when Mia first told her she was going to be spending a month in China. *I wish I could go. I've never left the country before.*

At the time, Mia had grumbled that the trip wasn't all Thea was making it out to be. But now, perched here on these stone steps, staring up the steep mountain slope, Mia felt a stirring of the wonder Thea had expressed all those weeks ago.

Here was something she'd never seen. Something she never *would* have seen in her little town back home.

Here was adventure—even if it wasn't exactly the sort of adventure she'd dreamed about.

Her ice pop was long gone by the time they reached Yongquan Temple. It seemed to appear out of nowhere, as if Mia had blinked and opened her eyes to find the temple dropped right out of the sky.

Mia and Jake grinned at each other in the muggy summer heat.

In that moment, things between them were the way they used to be—back when Jake used to build forts with her in the woods behind their house. When he'd been more than happy to go on adventures or play at being pirates—even if he always insisted on being captain, so Mia had to be first mate.

And there, standing tall and proud like sentinels on either side of a broad walkway, were the two Pottery Pagodas.

10

THE PAGODAS LOOKED A LITTLE DULL COMPARED
to the bright red temple building behind them. They
reminded Mia of the trunk she and Aunt Lin had
pulled from the closet. They were even worn in the
same way, some of their color chipped off to reveal
a pale white base. The paint that did remain was an
earthy brown-red.

Still, there was something regal and magnificent
about them. Each was five times as tall as Mia. Standing
beneath one, squinting upward against the sunlight to
see the intricate designs on the pagodas' gourd-shaped
crown, Mia felt very small and very young.

But that, according to Aunt Lin, was how history was

supposed to make you feel. Small and young and part of something much bigger than yourself.

Jake shielded his eyes from the sun too. "What was the clue again?"

Mia had it memorized. "'Jutting above the world on nine glazed layers, one thousand buddha chant in unison. Their voices are backed by the peal of heavenly bells. Listen to the ring of roaring lions—and find me above their cages.'"

The buddhas were certainly there. Bigger ones perched on the peaks of the pagodas' many eaves, some wearing little hats, others bald-headed. Tinier buddhas decorated the walls of each octagonal story. The "heavenly bells" were there too, hanging from each eave. But where were the lions?

Tourists and pilgrims swarmed the plaza in front of the pagodas, each trying to get a look, or snap a photograph, or just plunge deeper into the Yongquan Temple. There were at least two tour groups, and Mia tried to eavesdrop, half hoping she might hear something useful.

"These were built during the Song dynasty," one guide said, beckoning her group past Mia. "They're called the Thousand Buddha Pottery Pagoda, but there are actually one thousand and seventy-eight buddha, if you want to be exact. If you come closer, you can get a good look at the base of this pagoda. Etched into the pedestal are names of the pagoda's crafters. . . ."

The small red fence running around the pagodas meant no one could get too close, but Mia edged her way around the tour group to see the pedestal the guide was talking about. It wasn't easy, with so many other people struggling to do the same thing. Finally, Mia squeezed between two women and got to the front of the pack.

She pressed her stomach against the fence's upper railing as her eyes traced down the base of the pagoda. It was thicker around than the other levels, looking like an octagonal cauldron held up by little kneeling figures at each point. And on either side of each figure—lions! A ring of them encircled the pedestal, each with a unique, snarling face.

"Listen to the ring of roaring lions," Mia whispered to herself, "and find me above their cages."

The curved, geometric shapes containing each beast did look like cages. She reached for her messenger bag and rummaged for the copy of Zhu Yunwen's map—noting with some relief that the tour group was moving on. It left her and Jake with more privacy as she beckoned him toward her.

Together they scrutinized the map, then the pedestal, and then the map again. The lines leading up to the blank space beside each clue meant that only specific shapes would complete each section of the map.

"Look," Jake said, pointing. "See that curly, ace-of-spades-looking design stamped at the brim of the pedestal? Try that."

Mia obliged. It took a little fiddling before suddenly, and with such ease it might as well have been magic— or possibly destiny, or maybe just the *click* of something becoming right in the world—Mia got the shape on the pedestal to fit perfectly into the map.

She couldn't have stopped her shout of triumph if she'd wanted to.

One down.

Three more to go.

Mia figured they'd need to head back to the apartment immediately, to make it before their mom returned from her reunion. But when Jake caught her eyeing the other parts of the temple, a yearning tilt to her face, he took her by the shoulders and steered her up the ramp between the pagodas.

"Come on," he said, rolling his eyes. "We're not in that big of a hurry. Mom will be gone for hours."

Yongquan Temple spread out as pretty as a painting. Buildings rose around them, their red walls contrasted with white-rimmed windows. The edges of their dark roofs swooped down and then up again like four-pointed hats. Many had intricately decorated eaves, each adorned with swirling designs and colorful patterns.

Mia watched as an elderly gentleman clasped a stick of incense in his hands and bowed to a huge, golden Buddha statue sitting inside one of the temple buildings. A woman joined him, their knees resting against pillows to protect them from the hard temple floors.

Elsewhere, she and Jake ran into another statue, this one carved from glossy white marble. A tableau of flowers, fruits, and incense sat before it on a high table. Below it, lined up on a lower shelf, stood a procession of golden candles in wide-mouthed glass jars.

They reminded Mia of the row of candles she'd seen when she'd visited Lizbeth's church. *They're prayers,*

Lizbeth had told her when she'd asked about them. Mia wondered if these candles were prayers too.

A vender sold candles of different sizes nearby, and Mia toyed with the idea of buying one to light for Aunt Lin. But the thought of saying this aloud to Jake made her cringe with embarrassment, so she just walked on without saying a word.

The temple grounds opened onto a small pond. A white statue of a tall, slim figure rose from the center of it, surrounded by tree-reflecting waters and the tiny, round black shells of sunbathing turtles.

"Who's that supposed to be?" Jake asked, and seemed surprised when Mia answered, "Guanyin Pusa."

"And who's that?"

Mia narrowed her eyes at him, making sure he wasn't teasing her.

"She's like a goddess," she said. "She protects women and kids, and people pray to her when they want to have a baby."

Jake peered up at the swishing folds of her robes, at the crown and veil atop her hair. Her eyes were closed, peaceful, her mouth just barely curved in a smile.

"How do you know all that?" he said.

"You'd know it too, if you listened to Aunt Lin's stories more."

"Well, I don't hang out with her as much as you do," Jake said. To Mia's surprise, he didn't sound dismissive. In fact, he sounded almost wistful. When she looked up at him, though, he just laughed and poked his finger against her forehead, right between her eyes. "I've got better things to do."

Still, Mia knew what she'd heard. She mulled it over as they headed out of the temple and down the mountain toward the bus stop.

For most of her life, she'd wanted all the things Jake had that she didn't—a swarm of friends at school, a head for classes, an unshakable confidence that no one and nothing seemed able to dent.

It had never occurred to her that she might have things Jake envied too. It had especially never occurred to her that one of those things might be the time she spent with Aunt Lin.

"You know," she said, as they stood waiting for the bus to come. "You could hang out with me and Aunt Lin sometimes. I wouldn't mind."

"Sure, whatever," Jake said, and mussed up her hair.

*   *   *

They'd lingered longer than they'd meant to at Yongquan, and then it took more time than they'd expected for the bus to come, so by the time Mia and Jake reached the gate outside their apartment complex, they were a little concerned. They careened up the stairs—all five flights of them—and arrived, gasping and huffing, at their landing. Mia jabbed the doorbell.

"Is she back?" she whispered when her uncle opened the door, and slumped with relief when he shook his head.

They tumbled inside—had just barely slipped off their shoes when the doorbell rang again. Their mother blinked at them in surprise when they pulled the door open a second later.

"Were you two waiting by the door for me?" she said, laughing.

"They were eager for you to get home," Mia's uncle said. "How was your reunion?"

"It was lovely. It was like old times. And you? What did you three get up to?"

There was a brief silence. Then Mia's uncle shrugged. "I read my newspaper. Watched a little television." He grinned at Mia and Jake, his eyes twinkling. "And those two—they were so quiet, it was like they weren't even here."

11

WITH AUNT LIN GONE, MIA NO LONGER NEEDED
to sleep on the floor. But she would've gladly traded her
spot on the bed for Aunt Lin's safe return. The bedroom
felt strange without her, especially once the sun went
down. Unfamiliar noises drifted in from the open window:
lilting Chinese folk music from a neighbor's balcony ste-
reo, shouting from a nearby basketball court, cars swishing through streets still wet from the after-dinner rain.

Mia was accustomed to hearing nothing but cicadas
when she slept. She thought about closing the window,
but that would make the room too hot. There wasn't cen-
tral air-conditioning, and her mom wouldn't let her sleep
with the fan on, claiming it would give her a cold.

She distracted herself by reading the remaining treasure-map riddles instead:

> *Two brothers stand, eye to eye*
> *The fairer steady on the turtle's back*
> *Search for me low, on the heads of the darker brother's feet,*
> *Carved into a cheek like a scar*

That made about zero sense to her. She moved on to another unsolved riddle:

> *They came from the seas, murdering and pillaging*
> *Twenty thousand strong, like a battering wave*
> *But like a wave, they retreated again*
> *Driven by the sword of war's minister.*
> *Find me in the—*

"Mia?"

Mia stuffed the translated riddles beneath her blanket. "Yeah?"

Her mom smiled as she crossed the room. "You getting ready for bed?"

Mia shrugged, hoping her mom wouldn't come too

close and notice the riddles. She'd hidden her copy of the map—with the newly added piece from the Pottery Pagoda—deep at the bottom of her messenger bag, folded up beneath her compass. The original map, of course, lived on the flip side of the crane painting. Mia had slipped it into the desk drawer.

She still didn't have enough proof to tell her mom what she was doing. And right now, seeing the content smile on her face, Mia wouldn't have told her even if she thought she'd be believed.

Your mother is a little stressed right now, darling, Aunt Lin had told her once, when she was younger and suffering from some now long-forgotten slight at school. *How about you and I figure this out ourselves?*

She'd said similar things when Jake and Mia fought, or when Mia got upset because she was the only one parentless at a school function, or during those rare times when her mom lost her temper.

Your mother carries a lot on her shoulders, Aunt Lin would say. And even if Mia didn't always understand the specifics, she knew when her mom was tired or frazzled, even though her mom was good at hiding it.

Mia knew, despite all her complaining and feet-dragging, that this trip to China was really important to her mom. That she wouldn't want it ruined by anything.

So it was better that her mother didn't know.

Still, as her mother sat on the edge of Mia's bed and ran her fingers through Mia's hair, gently pulling tangles from the shower-damp strands, Mia wished that she could tell her everything. She leaned into her mother's touch, her heart filled with all the secrets she knew and couldn't say. They pressed so large inside her that it seemed impossible her mom couldn't tell.

"I'm going to take you and Jake someplace special tomorrow," her mom said. "It's called Sanfang Qixiang. Do you know what that means?"

"Three Something, Seven Something?" Mia guessed in English, translating the two words she recognized.

Since arriving in China, she'd more or less stuck to speaking Chinese all the time with everyone but Jake. It had seemed like the thing to do. But she was more accustomed to speaking like this with her mother back home, the two of them switching rapid-fire between English and Chinese, cobbling conversations—even sentences— together from a mishmash of words from each language.

Her mom laughed and answered in English too. "Yes,

pretty much. I guess you could call it 'Three Lanes and Seven Alleys.'"

"Why's it special?"

"It's a historic part of the city. There are buildings there that were first built in the Ming or Qing dynasties. You like that kind of stuff, right? I saw you and Aunt Lin brought Grandma's painting out of storage."

Mia stiffened. She peered up at her mom's face, trying to figure out if she suspected anything. "We were just looking at it."

"Your grandma used to say it might have been painted during the Ming dynasty." She laughed. "But who knows. That wasn't why she loved it so much. Her own mother—your great-grandmother—gave it to her as a wedding present. It was one of the few things she brought from her childhood home when she married."

Her fingers stilled in Mia's hair. She hesitated, then asked, "Are you sad that you never got to know your grandparents?"

Once, a very long time ago, she'd asked Mia a similar question about Mia's father. Mia did the same thing now as she'd done then. She shook her head and said, "I have you, and Jake, and Aunt Lin."

She would have said it a hundred times if it meant the crease of worry between her mother's eyes would go away. If it meant she'd smile.

Walking into Sanfang Qixiang from the rest of Fuzhou was like walking into an alternate dimension in the middle of the city. Skyscrapers rose in the distance, shimmering silver in the morning sunlight. The immediate landscape, however, was nothing but squat one- or two-story buildings.

Many were wooden, or had bare stone facades. Others bore a simple, clean wash of white paint, decorated by lattices of polished wood. Strings of cheerful red lanterns hung from their eaves, swaying in the breeze.

There were no cars, only a crush of people thronging the paved streets, and the stray passing of a rickshaw. It was like being pulled into the past, except for the modern clothing of their fellow tourists and—

"Is that really a Starbucks?" Jake said, laughing.

It really was.

Mia couldn't help giggling too. The coffee shop had at least tried to blend in, with fancy, old-fashioned wooden fretwork and some red lanterns, but there was no mistaking the Starbucks-green umbrellas outside the building. The people sipping from their cups up on the balcony didn't seem to mind the anachronism.

If Aunt Lin had been here, she might have *tsk*ed under her breath. Or she might have laughed and loved the strangeness of it.

"Come on," Mia's mom said, beckoning them deeper into the network of streets.

The next few hours were full of new, exciting things. They stumbled into a dim shop where an elderly man sold sheets of beautiful calligraphy that he'd write before your eyes. Farther down the street, a woman played erhu, a traditional Chinese instrument, her eyes closed and her bow singing across the strings as if it were pulling her and not the other way around.

Mia led the way to explore some *old*, exciting things too. They wandered through manicured gardens nestled beneath the shade of white walls, and stared at roofs that swooped like black raven's wings. Many of the ancient homes here were open to the public, each with a little placard on the wall explaining which family had once lived here so very long ago.

Their mom pointed out the special bricks making up

the building's walls. They were huge, and a pale, sandy color. "See the tiny seashells stuck in them?" she said. "It's because they're made out of sand collected from the nearby beaches."

It was all enough to almost—*almost*—make Mia forget about the unfinished map she'd hidden in her suitcase back at the apartment. The treasure she had to find. The aunt she needed to save.

"Where to next?" Jake said, after they'd found a dumpling shop to order lunch.

Their mom raised her eyebrows and fanned herself with a spare brochure. Even after hours tramping about in the muggy heat, she looked neat and put together—if perhaps a little boxed about the edges. Her thick, straight hair had started to slip from its bun. "Next, we eat and you let your old mother sit for a while."

But Mia was too full of fidgety energy to sit. Jake must have felt the same, because he only managed a minute or two in his chair before he jumped up again, tilting his head toward an antiques store a few shops down. "I'm going to check that out before the food comes."

Mia stayed slumped in her seat, her feet tapping

against the asphalt, until Jake turned to look at her over his shoulder.

"Aren't you coming?" he said, as if the invitation had been unspoken and obvious. As if he hadn't spent the last year snapping at Mia when she tried to follow along on things or assumed that he'd want to hang out.

She was out of her chair in two seconds, grinning.

"Don't be long," their mom shouted after them.

12

UNLIKE MANY OF THE OTHER SHOPS IN SANFANG
Qixiang, the antiques shop had its air-conditioning on
full blast. Mia shivered pleasantly. It was a relief to be out
of the heat for a bit, even if the day was growing increas-
ingly overcast. She hadn't realized how much she'd relied
on air-conditioning in the summer until she'd come to
China. A lot of places here still relied mostly on fans.

"Look at that," Jake whispered.

The store was a trove of trinkets and heirloom fur-
niture, but he went straight for a collection of antique
swords hanging off the back wall. Mia followed just a
breath behind.

The swords were all different shapes, one as straight

as a beam of moonlight, another arced like a silver hook. Jake glanced around to make sure no one was watching, then grinned at Mia and lifted the smallest sword from its rack. This one was still in its scabbard, so only the golden hilt showed, but he feinted a stab at her anyway.

Mia giggled and slapped her hands around an imaginary wound in her gut. She tilted backward onto a conveniently placed couch and was about to perform her best impression of a death spasm when a woman's voice cut through their antics. "*Hey*, you can't play around with that. And get up off that couch, child. It's older than your grandmother."

Mia scrambled onto her feet.

The storekeeper didn't lose her scowl. "These things are expensive," she snapped. "They're history, not foolish toys."

I know that, Mia thought. *I wouldn't ever think they were foolish.*

Jake spoke before she could, apologizing as he placed the sword back onto its rack. His Chinese wasn't as good as Mia's, but it didn't seem to matter. In a second he went from the laughing kid play-fighting with Mia to someone who was all maturity and deference and friendliness—contrite, but still confident. Smiling in a way that invited others to smile.

Mia tried to study him the way Lizbeth studied professional softball players, looking to perfect her swing. *You have to break it down*, she'd told Mia once. *Then put it all back together again.*

But this wasn't that easy. She couldn't put her finger on all the little things Jake did to be Jake. He just *was*.

The storekeeper, no matter how prickly, stood no chance. Her glower softened into a grudging smile.

"That sword you were holding," she said, "was once used to fight against pirates."

"Really?" Jake said, charming and charmed.

The woman's shoulders relaxed, just a touch. She gestured out toward the street—or maybe just at the rest of Sanfang Qixiang. "You've heard of Zhang Jing?"

Jake shook his head. Mia hadn't heard of Zhang Jing either, but it wouldn't have mattered anyway. The storekeeper was paying attention only to Jake.

"Was he a pirate?" he said.

"No, no. Zhang Jing was the minister of war in the . . . what was it? Ming dynasty? Late Ming dynasty. There were pirates attacking the Chinese coast at the time, plundering cities and wreaking havoc. He led a charge against them."

"Did he drive them away?" Mia asked.

There was a strange, tickling feeling in the back of her head. Like a memory trying to surface, or a thought struggling to form. She couldn't put her finger on what it was, but it had started when the storekeeper first said the word "pirates."

"He tried to. He fought some good battles. There was something like twenty thousand pirates at one point. They'd built strongholds along the coast—"

Mia didn't hear the rest of her sentence. Her mind had tripped on "twenty thousand"—had tripped and fallen right onto the thing that had been nudging against her thoughts:

They came from the seas, murdering and pillaging
Twenty thousand strong, like a battering wave
But like a wave, they retreated again
Driven by the sword of war's minister.
Find me in the—

She frowned, struggling to recall the rest. Find me in the *what*?

The storekeeper continued on about Zhang Jing,

oblivious: "He was very famous for it all—he has a house here. Are you two not from the city?"

"Oh, uh, no," Jake said. He met Mia's eyes, as if he knew exactly what she was trying to remember. "We're only visiting."

They came from the seas, murdering and pillaging
Twenty thousand strong, like a battering wave
But like a wave, they retreated again
Driven by the sword of war's minister.
Find me in the—

She almost had it. Teachers often got exasperated with Mia's memory—with all the spelling words she couldn't spell, with the directions she didn't follow, with the assignments she started and then forgot halfway through. Once, one had said, only half jokingly, *Mia, you could forget about your left shoe while pulling on your right.*

It wasn't entirely untrue. But only because Mia had very little interest in her shoes. The things she did care about, she focused on with great intensity. Right now, she tried to clear everything from her mind except for the words of the riddle.

But like a wave, they retreated again
Driven by the sword of war's minister.
Find me in the—
Find me in the southern heart of this lionheart's hearth.

"You said Zhang Jing had a house here?" Mia said, interrupting the storekeeper in the middle of a spiel about the city's landmarks. "In Sanfang Qixiang?"

The woman frowned at her. "I did."

Mia gave Jake a speaking look. "We need to go see it."

"Right," he said. He was already moving toward the door, his best, most polite smile pinned to his face. "Thanks so much for everything. I'm sorry about the trouble."

Mia didn't wait around to see how the storekeeper responded, just darted back into the streets. Her head buzzed with excitement.

First things first.

They needed to find a map.

13

FARTHER OUT FROM THE CENTER OF SANFANG
Qixiang, the buildings lost a little of their buffed shine,
but none of their character.

"Are you sure we're going in the right direction?"
Jake asked as they wended ever farther from the restaurant where they'd left their mother. He'd already asked
her twice.

Mia just nodded as she led the way down a nar-
row alley. The walls here were white too—but a dirt-
ier, moss-overgrown white. The lower portions were
stained with dirt and the passage of time. Unlike Sanfang
Qixiang's main streets, which seemed frozen in a strange,
half-modern, half-ancient alternate universe, time had

worn its way into the architecture here at the edges of the streets.

A soft rain began to fall, drizzling from the gray clouds.

"I'm serious, Mia," Jake said. "Mom's going to kill us if we—"

"Here," Mia said triumphantly. She blinked the rain from her eyelashes. "It's right here."

Jake sidled up next to her, trying to block the rain with his raised arm. Around them, the once-regular path had devolved into little more than the odd stone in the ground. Greenery grew in wild patches, encroaching on a crumbling building.

Parts of the wall bore traces of white paint. Other bits had worn clean through to the mortar—and others still were barely more than loose, clay brick. Pieces of the roof had fallen in, shattering on the ground into piles of rubble.

"This?" Jake said. "This is Zhang Jing's house?"

Mia picked her way closer to the building. The ground was uneven, the tall grass damp from the rain. It clung to her bare legs, wetting her socks.

"That's what it says," she said, pointing. Someone had

scrawled four Chinese characters on the bare wall, the red words stark against the gray bricks. "'Zhang Jing's house.'"

The characters were right next to a doorway—a doorway with a pair of cracked and faded doors. Two dusty lanterns hung above the threshold. The city, Mia's mom had explained, had taken a lot of care recently to renovate this area—to preserve a little of the past. But barely any care, it seemed, had been taken here.

Would Zhu Yunwen's clue still exist? Or would it, too, have crumbled during the intervening years?

A stick snapped behind Mia. She turned to look at Jake—then realized that Jake was on her other side, poking around a thatch of grass. So who had been behind her?

"Well, this is the southern side of the house," Jake said. "What was the last line again? 'Find me in the southern heart of this lionheart's hearth.' So the clue has to be around here somewhere."

Mia looked back to the house. Despite its state, it still bore the grandiosity of age and size. She tilted her head, imagining away the gaps in the wall, filling in the roof and restoring the doors to the deep, polished red they must have been once upon a time. This had been a minister's house. It would have had parlors and silk screens, and perhaps a peaceful garden of manicured greenery.

Important people—people with the power to shift and mold history—would have gathered beneath its roof to sip tea and make plans. Mia felt their ghosts pressing around her.

Or maybe it wasn't ghosts at all. She whirled around again, the back of her neck prickling, her ears straining. She *swore* she'd heard something. And this time, she thought she'd seen something too—a flash of movement at the corner of her vision.

"Someone's watching us," she whispered.

"Hmm?" Jake squatted beside a bit of crumbled wall, picking at the fallen bricks. "What do you think the riddle means by 'the southern heart'? Should we head inside?"

One of the doors was cracked open—not exactly inviting, but suggesting that visitors were allowed to enter.

Mia hesitated, checking over her shoulder. By the time she turned back again, Jake was halfway through the door. She hurried to keep up.

To her surprise, the door didn't lead to a room, but straight into a courtyard. A clothesline was strung across one edge of it. It was currently bare of actual clothing—someone must have taken them down in anticipation of the rain—but the hangers were still there. Proof that someone actually lived here.

More proof lay around the courtyard in the form of little plastic chairs and other knickknacks. A birdcage hung beneath one of the eaves. A bicycle leaned against the wall, a plastic bag tied around the seat to keep it dry.

Mia relaxed a little. She'd probably just heard the footsteps of a resident—someone trying to get out of the rain. It was coming down harder now. She and Jake ducked beneath an overhang.

"Maybe the courtyard is supposed to be the heart?" Mia said, looking around. It did seem to be in the middle of everything. She sighed. "I didn't bring the map."

Without the aid of the map's guiding lines, it would be a whole lot harder to make sure they'd found the right missing piece.

Jake looked vaguely embarrassed as he reached into his pocket. "I did."

"You *did*?"

"It turned out to be the right decision, didn't it?" he said defensively. He unfolded the sheet of paper and pressed it flat against one of the wooden walls. Together, they studied the blank space they were supposed to be filling in from the "southern heart" of Zhang Jing's home.

Mia turned to face the threshold they'd just crossed. If the courtyard was the heart of the compound, then this made sense as the southern side of the heart. She studied the plain, ancient walls, searching for something like the pattern she'd found at the base of the Pottery Pagoda. There was nothing to be seen.

Maybe she'd gotten the cardinal directions mixed up. The sky was too overcast to look to the sun for clues—and besides, it was too near noon for that. She chewed at her bottom lip and stepped deeper into the courtyard, ready to investigate every inch of it for Zhu Yunwen's clue.

She didn't get far before something arrested her attention. But it wasn't a pattern or a clue. It was a face peering at her from one of the compound's latticed windows.

It belonged to a girl a little younger than herself, her dark eyes curious. Mia stared back, just as intrigued.

The other girl opened her mouth, as if to speak. Then her gaze flickered up and past Mia's head. Her eyes widened.

This time Mia whirled around so quickly she almost

lost her balance. She was just fast enough to catch what the girl had seen—

A bear of a man with a head of hair like black thunder-clouds.

Ying.

It was Ying.

Her heart pounded.

He stood in the doorway of the southern wall, some-thing pale blue in his hands. He looked raggedy, like he hadn't slept since she'd last seen him. His eyes met hers, just for a second. They were dark, and still, and filled with the same muddy mix of melancholy and irritation Mia had shied away from when he'd come to tea.

Then her gaze shifted back to his hands, and she realized what he was holding.

That blue was the blue of Aunt Lin's notebook. The robin's egg of its inside pages.

Was this the missing page?

The one Aunt Lin had used to copy the map?

Where is she? Mia tried to shout. *Where's Aunt Lin?*

But her lungs wouldn't expand, and her lips wouldn't move, and finally, all she could manage was to turn to Jake—Jake, who was crouched by the corner where the southern wall met the west, his back to her—and cry his name.

"Look!" she said, when his head came up.

"Just a second," he said. "I've found something—"

"Jake—it's Ying!"

He stood and looked. But it was too late. The man had gone, leaving the doorway empty but for the drizzle and the dampening grass. Mia's legs unfroze. She tore out of the compound, searching for a flash of Ying's dark hair. For a glimpse of that blue notebook paper.

The path outside lay just as abandoned.

Where had he gone?

Was Aunt Lin nearby too? Was she desperately trying to get Mia's attention right this moment?

She startled as someone's hand closed around her shoulder. It was only Jake, his eyes bright with excitement. "I think I found it," he said. "The clue."

Mia resisted as he tried to pull her back into the courtyard. "I saw Ying—I swear I did."

"Well, he's not here." Jake barely sounded like he was listening to her. He'd learned, at least, to not say things like, *You thought you saw him, Mia*, which was what he used to say. It had driven Mia absolutely crazy.

But she could tell that was what he was thinking.

"Come here," he said, and sighed when she ripped out of his grasp, darting forward a few more steps.

"Aunt Lin!" she shouted into the rain. *"Aunt Lin!"*

"Mia," Jake snapped. "There's no one there."

Mia sucked in a long breath and quieted. He was right. There was no one there—not anymore. But there had been. The shock of it reverberated in her.

Jake took hold of her shoulder again, and this time she didn't resist, grudgingly following him back into the courtyard. As it turned out, he hadn't been looking at the wall, but at a pile of loose bricks that had fallen off it. Someone had collected them into a stack.

Jake grabbed one and held it up for Mia to examine. "See it?"

The brick must have cracked in half when it fell, leaving one end rough with protruding stones. No, they weren't stone—they were tiny seashells. Mia remembered what her mother had said about the houses here being built from sand.

But none of that felt relevant right now. Not with Ying's shadow hanging over her.

"Yeah, shells," she said. "So what?"

Jake gave her an exasperated look, dropped the brick, and picked up another one. This one was less damaged. He tilted it toward the weak sunlight, so that the shells glittered. "You don't see it? There's a pattern there!"

Mia squinted. Once she managed to pull her thoughts from Ying and actually focus on the brick, she did see what Jake was talking about. The shells embedded in the brick weren't randomly scattered, as she'd thought. They'd been placed to form a pattern. It looked a bit like a cross, only with an additional line at the end of it.

"Are they all like this?" Mia tilted her head back to look at the rest of the wall.

"I think most of them are." Jake grinned at her, his annoyance momentarily forgotten. "Can you imagine the work it must have taken, making every single brick like this?"

Mia shrugged. She couldn't help checking over her shoulder again, just to make sure Ying wasn't lurking. She almost wished he *were*—then at least Jake might see him.

She stayed quiet as Jake copied the new clue onto their map. He folded it back up afterward and stuck it in his pocket with a smile. "Two clues in two days. Not bad."

Mia didn't smile back. "I saw him, Jake," she said quietly. "I saw Ying. He was right there."

"You sure you're not just saying that because you're upset I found the clue and you didn't?" Jake said, laughing.

"Yes, I'm sure," Mia growled. "I *saw* him—"

"Okay, okay." Jake's grin faded. "Don't freak out."

I'm not freaking out, she thought. But saying it would only make things worse. So Mia just bit her tongue, silent, and looked away. Her chest tightened.

Jake motioned for her to lead the way out of the compound. "I'm just saying, it would be a pretty big coincidence, you know? Him being here exactly the same moment we're here. Even if you're right about him having the map and the clues. Even if you're right about him trying to find the treasure—the chances of him showing up here . . ."

Mia walked faster, trying to leave her brother and his doubts behind.

At the end of the day, when push came to shove, Jake would never take her seriously.

14

THEY DIDN'T STAY MUCH LONGER AT SANFANG
Qixiang after that. Between the rain and the new, crackly, thunderclap tension between Mia and Jake, there wasn't much fun left in it. Their mom wasn't in the best of moods either. She'd been left alone at the table for twenty minutes with plates of rapidly cooling dumplings.

"I don't know what got into you two." She sighed as they waited for the bus to take them home.

Neither Mia nor Jake replied.

The rain got harder as the afternoon wore on, crashing onto the city in waves of water. Mia holed up in Aunt Lin's room, trying to read one of the books she'd brought, and wishing that the rain would stop so she could go outside. That Jake would come and apologize for being an idiot and not believing her.

That her aunt had never disappeared.

Just before sunset, one of three of her wishes came true: The rain slowed to a sprinkle, then dwindled away entirely. Mia looked up hopefully when Jake knocked at her door, but he didn't look her in the eye, and only said, "Come on, Mom wants us to pick up some stuff for dinner before it gets dark."

The two of them were quiet as they headed down the stairs. Outside, the sunlight had turned golden, the air cooled by the afternoon showers. Mia was lost in her thoughts, sidestepping puddles, and didn't notice Jake wandering away from her until he was on the other side of the parking lot.

He edged up to the fence surrounding the basketball court. On the other side, a group of boys—high school age, maybe a little older than him—ran a big, spongy roller across the court, trying to soak up the rainwater.

Mia came up behind him, was about to tell him they needed to go, when one of the other boys caught sight of them.

"Hey," he said. "Do you play?"

Jake gave him an easy grin. The one that made him everyone's friend in two seconds flat. "Sure," he said. "Are you looking for someone to join you guys?"

The older boy called back to his friends, and before Mia knew it, Jake had jogged onto the damp court—was laughing and chatting with the other boys. She herself might as well have been a ghost on the other side of the fence. Or perhaps just part of the scenery.

When Jake finally remembered that she existed, he only said, "Can you go on without me? You know where the store is, right?"

Mia nodded. She tried to say something—*what*, she wasn't sure. *Something.* But it didn't matter what it was, because Jake never gave her the chance. He turned back to the other boys, and they closed themselves off to her, lit by the tall lights of the basketball court.

She waited a few seconds longer, as if Jake might change his mind. Then she slunk off alone down the street.

By the time she returned from the store, swinging a bag of groceries, the basketball game was underway. She snuck looks at the court as she passed, and couldn't help noting that Jake was just as good, if not better, than most of the other players. She disappeared into the apartment building just as he made a basket. The boys' cheers swelled the twilight darkness.

"Oh, that's nice," their mom said, when Mia handed her the groceries and told her Jake was still outside. "He's always quick to make friends, isn't he?"

"Yeah," Mia said. "I guess."

She stayed a little longer in the kitchen, helping her mom wash vegetables and peel sweet potatoes. But then her uncle came in to lend a hand, and the space wasn't large enough for three people, even if the third was as small as Mia. She retreated back to Aunt Lin's room, and her book, and the two wishes she'd wished that hadn't come true.

The weekend arrived. A few weeks ago, when Mia had been at home and school had been in session, this would have been cause for celebration. Now it was just cause for boredom.

Jake seemed to have forgotten all about Mia, and the treasure hunt, and everything they'd been working for. When he wasn't in the middle of an actual game, he was playing one-on-one keep-away or throwing hoops by himself. He came home sweaty and exhausted, barely pausing to wolf down food before showering and collapsing onto the sofa. At dinner, he and their uncle—who'd apparently loved to play basketball, too, when he was younger—went on about basketball in a language Mia only half understood.

The whole situation wouldn't have been so awful if she were doing better with the last two riddles. But each was as indecipherable as the other, and there were only so many times Mia could reread them before she just wanted to bang her head against the wall.

Sunday morning, her mom declared that she and Mia were going clothing shopping. She seemed to expect Mia to be more excited about that than Mia really was. For her sake, Mia tried to pretend.

They caught a bus downtown and trudged through one bright, shiny shopping mall after another. The malls here were much bigger than any in Mia's little hometown, but otherwise they were pretty similar. The familiarity was more tiresome than it was comforting.

Usually, Aunt Lin took Mia shopping if she needed clothing. Or, more recently, Mia would go with Thea and Lizbeth. Coming to this mall with her mom was a bit strange.

She let her mother hustle her from store to store. She slipped into dresses, then out again—pulled on shirts and jackets and then shimmied them off again. Every time her mom said, "Do you like it?" she just shrugged, and her mom would sigh.

"Okay, Mia," she said after an hour or two had passed. They stood by the escalators in a department store, and Mia stared at the people getting on and off, knowing what question was coming next. "What's wrong?"

My job is to put out fires, her mom had said once, when Mia asked her what she did at work. Mia was accustomed to her taking work calls on weekends or running into the office after dinner because some business catastrophe or another had thrown everyone into a panic.

Most times, Mia enjoyed knowing that people needed her mom—that they looked to her to solve their problems. Other times, she wished her mom were as good at understanding Mia's catastrophes as she was those of her company.

"Mia?"

"Nothing," Mia said.

"Doesn't seem like nothing," her mom said, and Mia didn't really have a response to that, so she just looked back at her and shrugged. When her mom spoke again, her voice was softer. A little thin. "Is this about Aunt Lin being gone?"

It was, but not in the way she thought. Not in any way Mia could tell her.

Her mother smiled, and for once it wasn't perfect. It wasn't even nice. It fluttered around her mouth like something wounded. "It doesn't have to be that terrible. I thought it might give us some time to spend together—just us. Mia, I know we don't always get a lot of time with each other when we're at home. I'm sorry about that."

It felt wrong to hear her mother apologize. It felt even more wrong to see her upset and trying to hide it and failing.

It's okay, Mia tried to say, but couldn't, so she just stared at the ground instead.

"Mia, you know Aunt Lin isn't—she isn't always reliable." Her mouth tightened, like she regretted saying that, but it didn't stop the sudden anger in Mia's stomach.

"She is," she bit out. "She—"

She cut herself off. There were a lot of ways she could

finish that sentence. A lot of hurtful things she could say—that roiled around in her head, burning like steam. But she saw the way her mom's face had gone quiet and still, and she swallowed everything back.

They stood in silence for a little while.

"Do you want to go home?" Mia's mom said finally.

Mia knew her mom meant the apartment and not *home* home. But when she nodded, she knew in her heart that she meant the latter.

15

BACK AT THE APARTMENT, MIA'S MOM SILENTLY
disappeared into her room with her laptop. Her brow was
furrowed. Whether it was because of their fight at the
department store, or because of the work call she'd received
just as they came through the door, Mia wasn't sure. It was
eight a.m. on a Sunday back home, and her mom was tech-
nically on vacation, so something big must have happened.

As "fire putter-outer," Mia's mom was never really off
from work. Not completely. *Getting this month away wasn't*
easy for her, Aunt Lin had told Mia, gently chiding, when
she'd heard her complaining about how long they'd be
in China. *It was really important to her to have this time with you*
and Jake.

Mia had forgotten that conversation until now, and she didn't like the way it made her stomach twist. She looked toward her mother's closed door. It was too late to do anything now. She could already hear her mom speaking to someone in English on the telephone.

"Didn't find anything you liked?"

Mia hadn't even noticed her uncle hanging out on the sofa, his ever-present newspaper half blocking his face. He lowered it as she turned to face him.

Mia shrugged. "Not really. Is Jake home?"

"Not yet," he said. "Your brother really loves basketball, doesn't he?"

"Even more than he likes soccer."

"What sort of things do you like to do?" he asked her. "Do you play any sports? Your mother used to love running track."

Lizbeth was the sporty one of Mia's trio of friends. Thea rode horses and wanted to compete more now that she was older, but Lizbeth was the one who'd played soccer since she was old enough to kick a ball and was, as even Jake admitted, a fiend on the softball pitch.

When Mia played sports in PE, she found her thoughts drifting halfway through games. Besides, what point was there in trying when Jake was already better? He'd claimed the ball field as his territory before Mia had ever had a chance.

She shrugged. "Sometimes I play."

She'd already started turning away when she got an idea.

"Riddles," she said. "I like solving riddles."

"What sorts of riddles?"

"All kinds. I'm working on one now." She hesitated. "Do you want to help me?"

Her uncle set his newspaper aside and smiled. "Of course." He tapped the side of his head. "As much help as this old brain can give you, anyway. What's this riddle?"

Mia closed her eyes and let the first riddle float to the top of her memory. After so many rereads, it wasn't hard. Then she realized that she had memorized the riddle in English. Awkwardly, she translated it back into Chinese.

"'Two brothers stand, eye to eye, the fairer steady on the turtle's back. Search for me low, on the heads of the darker brother's feet, carved into a cheek like a scar.'"

She looked at her uncle anxiously when she was done, hoping he wouldn't laugh at her or her shaky translation.

"The answer is supposed to be a place around here, I think."

"Hmm." He tilted his head and fiddled with his horn-rimmed reading glasses. "Two brothers? It sounds like it's talking about statues of some kind."

Mia nodded. "And one of them is standing on a turtle's back. Do you know any statues like that?"

His forehead wrinkled. "I'm afraid not."

Mia tried to hide her disappointment, but she'd never been very good at concealing her emotions. They slipped out in the downward quirk of her mouth, in the pull of her brows and the flicker in her eyes.

"Hey, hey," her uncle said. "We've only just begun. You can't lose hope so quickly. Let's break this riddle apart. Where should we begin?"

"The turtle," Mia said. "That's the weirdest part."

"A brother on a turtle's back," her uncle mused.

"The *darker* brother."

"Yes, the—" A spark lit in her uncle's eyes. "Wait. What if the riddle isn't talking about people, or statues, but about buildings? Go fetch those brochures I gave you."

Mia ran to get them. When she came back, her uncle splayed them out on the coffee table and shuffled through them. He jabbed his finger at a photograph of a gleaming white tower. "There it is! The White Pagoda."

Mia frowned, trying to piece things together. "So?"

"So," her uncle said, pushing the brochure toward her, "read what it says in there. Does it tell you where the White Pagoda is located? I'm afraid my English isn't very good."

Mia sped through the brochure until she found her answer. "It's on a mountain," she said slowly, translating aloud as she read, "called Yushan, which, from a distance, looks like—" She looked up, meeting her uncle's twinkling eyes. "Looks like a giant turtle."

"I think we've solved half your riddle," he said.

"But how can a pagoda have a brother?"

"A *darker* brother," her uncle reminded her, inflecting the word just as she had. He flipped to the last page in the White Pagoda's brochure. There, a small paragraph encouraged tourists to visit Wushi Mountain, as well, where—

Mia was grinning before she got to the last word. "They're twin pagodas," she said. "The white one on Yushan, and the black one."

Her uncle winked. "And so you have your answer.

Well, almost. What do you think of the last part of the riddle? The bit about searching for 'me' low, and something carved into a cheek like a scar?"

"Oh," Mia said, stumbling on her reply, "I don't think that bit's important. It's just— I might have translated it wrong."

"I see." He obviously didn't believe her, and Mia flushed, but he didn't press. He just laughed and said, "Are you going to be running off again, Mia?"

Mia flushed even deeper.

Her uncle turned hesitant too. He worked his next words around in his mouth a little before speaking them. "Do you want me to come with you to Wushi Mountain? It's been a long time since I've been there, but I could still show you around, if you wanted."

"I—" Mia said. "I think I'm going to go with Jake."

For a second, he looked so disappointed that Mia wished she could take her answer back. Except, how could she properly look for the clue with her uncle around? Helping her solve the riddle was one thing. If he came with her to Wushi Mountain and watched her search for the missing pattern, he'd have to realize that something bigger was going on.

"But only next time your mom's distracted? What are you two up to, Mia?"

"Nothing." Mia hurried to her feet, the White Pagoda brochure folded up in her hands. She flashed her uncle what she hoped was a breezy smile. "Nothing at all."

16

THE WORK CATASTROPHE, WHATEVER IT
was, must have kept Mia's mother up all night, because
she didn't get out of bed the next day until nearly noon.
Even then, she seemed only half awake. She'd gotten
invited to an early dinner with another group of friends,
but she seemed less excited about it this time.

"To be honest," Mia heard her say to her uncle, "I'm
afraid I'll fall asleep during a toast."

But five o'clock found her gamely in front of her van-
ity mirror, slipping in her earrings. Mia sat cross-legged
on the bed behind her.

"Are you sure you don't want to come with me?" her

mom asked. "It could be fun. It's supposed to be a really nice restaurant."

Mia shrugged. "That's okay. I'll just stay home."

Her mom gave Mia's reflection a small, tired smile. "All right."

They hadn't spoken, not really, since they'd argued at the mall, and for just a moment Mia almost changed her mind—almost said, *Actually, I do want to go—take me with you.*

If her mom had asked again, she might have. But she didn't, and so Mia just watched her leave.

She waited five, ten, fifteen minutes. Long enough to be sure that her mom's ride had whisked her away. Then she, too, pulled on her shoes and hurried down the stairs.

She didn't actually have any plans of staying home.

Not when there was a clue to collect.

Mia heard the thumping of Jake's basketball game even before she'd shut the apartment complex's heavy outer door. There came the satisfying noise of a ball whooshing through nothing but net and the whoops of the scoring team. Mia fiddled with the strap of her messenger bag.

Jake would want to come with her for this, wouldn't he? They'd started this expedition together, and it only seemed right to continue it together.

Her feet brought her to the edge of the basketball court. The game had paused to give the teams time to plan their next play—or maybe to just crack jokes and pound each other on the back, which was what they seemed to be doing. Jake fit in as well as he fit in anywhere—which was to say, perfectly.

Mia imagined herself clinking open the door in the tall, chain-link fence. Imagined herself walking step by ponderous step to the middle of the court, waiting awkwardly for Jake or one of the other boys to stop laughing long enough to notice her. Then what? She'd have to ask Jake to stop in the middle of his game to come to Wushi Mountain with her.

She rolled the question around in her head and couldn't come up with a way to arrange the words so they didn't make her sound like a child. Like a little kid who still needed her big brother to take her places.

Her pride bristled.

She turned on her heel and headed, alone, for the bus stop.

But she couldn't help hoping that Jake might notice her after all. She couldn't help her ears straining—even after the game started up again and everything was drowned out by the thump of the basketball, the squeak of sneakers against pavement—for Jake calling out her name.

Like their mother, he never did.

Never mind, Mia told herself firmly. She'd always known she was different from Jake, and different from their mother. She'd always known they didn't understand the things that were important to her—not the way Aunt Lin did. She didn't need them to.

Until she rescued Aunt Lin, she'd be fine on her own.

As Mia climbed aboard the bus to the Black Pagoda, she half expected the driver to ask her where she was going or if she was really traveling alone. Adults were always telling her she looked young for her age, and it wasn't uncommon for store clerks or library workers to worry that Mia had gotten separated from her parents.

Luckily, the bus driver only glanced at her before turning back to the road. Maybe he didn't think it strange that a little girl would travel by herself. Or maybe he thought she was attached to the lady who boarded before her, or was traveling with the man who boarded behind.

Either way, Mia encountered no trouble as she made her way to the back of the bus. There was an empty seat beside a sniffly young woman wearing a face mask. Mia took it when it became obvious that no one else was interested. It was hard to feel excited, the way she had during the bus rides to Gushan or to the Sanfang Qixiang district. Mostly, she just felt alone.

Wushi Mountain—or at least the foot of it, where the Black Pagoda stood—wasn't full of trees and natural scenery the way Gushan had been. In fact, it didn't look much different from the rest of the city. And the Black Pagoda, Mia discovered as she peered out the bus window, was far taller than the Pottery Pagodas. It shot up above the lower buildings around it, seven grand stories of dark gray granite crowned by a black roof and a spiraling pinnacle.

The long summer days meant that the evening sun still glinted off the surrounding skyscrapers, but the Black Pagoda soaked in the yellow light like a cold-blooded snake. There was something distinctly scalelike about the black ridges on its roofs. It gave the impression of an enormous, slumbering dragon wrapped around the tower, its head tucked out of sight.

It was a quiet evening. Mia found herself one of only a few people milling about the tower's base. She waited for a young couple to wander off, holding hands, before pulling her copy of Zhu Yunwen's map from her messenger bag.

She went over the riddle again in her head, just to make sure she had everything straight:

> Two brothers stand, eye to eye
> The fairer steady on the turtle's back
> Search for me low, on the heads of the darker brother's feet,
> Carved into a cheek like a scar.

"Darker brother's feet" had turned out to be metaphoric. But what about "cheek"? Mia stepped past the opening in the little stone fence ringing the tower's base. There were stone figures carved at each corner of the pagoda. Each stood almost as tall as she did, their faces serene, their hands clasped around sheathed swords—or maybe they were scepters. The worn stone made it hard to tell.

Mia ran her fingers over the warm, rough stone. Then she frowned. There was something off about the stone relief—something not quite right about its head. She propped herself up on tiptoe to reach its face, feeling the difference in the stone.

Effort had been made to make things blend in, but the stone composing the figure's head seemed a little smoother. A little newer.

"You noticed too?" a voice called out.

The couple was back, hovering just beyond the stone fence. The man smiled at her. He was the one who'd spoken.

Mia blinked at him.

"The heads," the man said. His left hand was entangled with that of the woman next to him, but he waved his right one at the stone-relief statues. "They used to all be broken off, but the city recently repaired them. They say they look the way they used to now, but who knows? I think they're a little off."

"Hush," his girlfriend said, fond and chiding. "She didn't ask for a history lesson."

"Maybe she likes history," the man protested, laughing. But he turned from Mia as he spoke, and the two of them wandered away, lost in each other, before Mia could say *yes*, yes she did—couldn't he tell her more?

Alone now, she circled the base of the tower. Each of the figures had the same *off*ness about their heads and faces. Had they really been broken off, once upon a time, like the man said?

"Carved into a cheek like a scar," the riddle said. What if the restorers hadn't made the heads exactly as they'd been before and the clue was gone? Mia's fingers tightened around her messenger bag, twisting the strap in her hands. It seemed heavier than it had just moments ago. Everything seemed heavier—her chest, her feet, the hot, humid air.

The horizon ignited red and yellow with sunset. Mia had set out later than she should have, and now she didn't have enough time to properly study the pagoda before night fell. She didn't know how late the buses ran. What if she missed the last one? She didn't have enough money for a taxi.

She backed away from the tower, torn. If she left without the clue, who knew when she'd be able to return?

But she didn't like the idea of wandering about the city at night, alone and without even a cell phone.

So she made one last trip around the tower, searching desperately for any sign of Zhu Yunwen's clue.

Then, heavyhearted, she headed back to the bus stop.

17

LUCKILY, THE BUSES WERE STILL RUNNING.
Mia's jolt of relief didn't last long, though. By the time she got off at the stop near the apartment, her mood was as gloomy as the murky twilight. She walked with her eyes on the pavement and hardly noticed the other people sharing the sidewalk until one nearly ran into her.

"Mia!" he said. Mia looked up.

It was her uncle. They stood outside a small restaurant, both of them bathed in yellow lamplight and the sizzling smell of day-old oil.

"I was getting worried," her uncle said. He wasn't angry, as her mother would have been, or gently chiding, as Aunt Lin would have been. Mostly, he sounded relieved.

"I'm sorry." Mia scuffed her shoe against the pavement, and for a long moment, neither of them spoke or moved. "Is my mom home?"

"Not yet," he said.

Another moment passed, this one interrupted only when they shuffled aside to let someone exit the restaurant.

"Well," Mia's uncle said finally, "you caught me on my way to the store. Want to come with me, if you aren't tired?"

Mia nodded, and they fell into step together. The streets were lively even after sundown, people taking advantage of the cooler temperatures. They strolled toward the river, which stretched dark and mysterious into the distance, lit only in glinting patches by the city lights.

"Did you enjoy your trip to the Black Pagoda?" he asked.

There was no point in pretending that that wasn't where she'd run off to.

"I guess."

That was all she'd planned to say, but her uncle glanced down at her and seemed to expect more. A

few days ago, she might have stayed quiet anyway. But
he had helped her solve the riddle in the first place, so
maybe she owed him a little more. Besides, it felt nice to
have someone to talk to.

"There was something I wanted to see that was
destroyed—at the bottom of the pagoda," she added
when he raised his eyebrow. She gestured with her
hands. "There are those stone figures, right? But a lot of
them had their heads smashed off."

"Ah," he said. "I do remember that, actually. Aren't
they renovating them now, though? Most of them should
be repaired."

"I wanted to see the originals," Mia said, and he
laughed.

"You sound just like your aunt."

Mia smiled, too. It was something she could imagine
Aunt Lin saying. Her aunt had loved visiting museums
and historic sites. *Can you imagine?* she'd say, her feet
planted in the aisle of an ancient church. *Think of all the
things that have happened here. All the other people who came here
before us.* She understood when things weren't exactly the
way they used to be—sometimes old things needed to
be restored or repaired. But nothing made her eyes light

up like something that had survived the centuries intact and untouched.

"Do you know how the statues got damaged?" Mia said.

"You know, I think I remember someone telling me that it happened during the Cultural Revolution. I don't know the details. A lot of things were destroyed back then—especially historic places."

"Why?"

The Chinese Cultural Revolution shaded the background of Aunt Lin's stories about her childhood. She mentioned it when talking about the books that had been banned, or the patriotic songs they'd learned in school, or the ration tickets she'd needed to buy necessities like food or cloth. It was the reason she'd gone to do farm work in the countryside—where she'd met Ying and found Zhu Yunwen's well.

But despite all the bits and pieces Mia had heard about the Cultural Revolution, she'd never truly understood it. It wasn't like the history that was taught in school, summarized into reading chapters and monthly quizzes. It seemed bigger. Messier.

Real history, Aunt Lin always said, was like that. Big

and messy and complicated. She'd tap on the covers of Mia's history books and say, *That's only the simplified version. That's just touching the surface.*

But Mia's classes at school had never talked about the Chinese Cultural Revolution, so she'd never even gotten a simplified, touching-the-surface version of events. Instead, she'd received stories of a life lived.

"Why did they destroy historic things?" her uncle mused to himself. He hesitated, taking a minute to think. "The Cultural Revolution was supposed to make China more modern—more developed. People believed that sticking to old traditions and old ways of thought were suffocating the country's progress. A lot of people got swept up in the fervor and did things that don't seem to make any sense now. Like breaking historic things as a symbolic gesture."

"And now we can't get any of it back." Frustration made Mia's words clipped. She needed this clue. She needed to find this treasure. She needed to save Aunt Lin.

And now it seemed history itself—once a mysterious and beckoning friend—was conspiring against her.

"You really are just like your aunt," Mia's uncle said.

He laughed, and that should have rankled Mia's nerves, but he sounded so fond that she couldn't quite manage it. "Sometimes bits of history are lost, Mia—whether it's because people destroyed it, or because it just got old and forgotten and worn away."

"Not if we save it."

"Can you save everything?" he said. "Oh, here's the store. We almost missed it."

It was an easy place to miss—just a few square yards of scuffed laminate floor and pale, fluorescent lights. The woman behind the checkout counter smiled at Mia's uncle like they knew each other.

"Anything you want to pick up while we're here?" he asked Mia, who shook her head. Mostly, she just wanted to get home, and climb into bed, and curl around her disappointment.

Her uncle, however, seemed set on taking his time. He wandered through the cramped aisles as if he might find treasure in them. Mia wasn't even sure what he'd come to get.

It probably wasn't the small pile of sparklers and fireworks he stopped in front of, his face splitting into a grin. He beckoned Mia closer. "Do you know what these are?"

"We have fireworks in America," she said, only half joking.

"I used to love these as a kid." He dug around the pile, and picked out a little one, barely the length of Mia's hand. It looked like a miniature rocket. "Especially these. They shoot right up into the air. We used to compete to see who could get theirs higher. I'm surprised they're selling them now—usually it's more of a New Year's sort of thing. Maybe it's a sign."

"A sign of what?"

He smiled. "A sign that we should buy it. Do you want one?"

Mia looked at it doubtfully. "I don't think I could bring it on the plane."

"Then we'll have to set it off before you go," he said.

They brought it to the checkout counter along with some milk and a bag of sunflower seeds. Mia's uncle had just paid when his cell phone rang.

"One second, I think this is your brother—" He motioned for Mia to grab the rocket while he took the other bag. "Hello? Yes, I found her. She's fine." A pause. "We're just at the store. We'll be home soon."

"Did he finish his basketball game?" Mia asked once

her uncle had hung up. She tried to keep the question casual, like it didn't matter to her one way or another.

"Oh, he finished that a while back," her uncle replied. "He stopped playing once we realized you were missing. I think he was a little worried."

"He doesn't need to worry," Mia said automatically. "I don't always have to go places with him."

"Maybe that's what has him worried. You not needing him to take you places anymore."

Mia laughed at the idea. "Jake barely wants to hang out with me anymore. I don't think he's worried about anything."

Her uncle gave her a considering look. "Has Aunt Lin told you stories about us, when we were growing up?"

"A little," Mia said. When Aunt Lin had recounted tales of her childhood here in Fuzhou, she'd mostly talked about the adventures she'd gotten up to with her school friends, or with Mia's mother, once she was old enough to take around the city. She'd mentioned her other two siblings too—Mia's uncle and second aunt— but less frequently. "She said you guys played with your own friends more than with each other."

"That's true," her uncle said. "Once we got older, we

each had our own gang of friends. But when we were small, I wanted to follow her everywhere. And we got up to some pretty crazy things."

"Like what?"

He grinned. "Come on, let's head homeward, and I'll tell you on the way."

18

IT WAS GETTING TO BE FULL DARK AS THE TWO of them headed back to the apartment. The basketball court lay empty, the stadium lights extinguished. That same neighbor, somewhere up on the fifth or sixth floor, now blasted pop music from their balcony radio. It was a nice change, Mia figured, from the folk music they usually played at night.

"In some ways, your Aunt Lin was just like she is now, when she was younger," Mia's uncle said. "Especially before your mom and little aunt were born, when it was just the two of us. She was always tearing off on adventures—things so crazy and stupid dangerous that none of her friends would go along. Only I would, because I wanted so badly to keep up with her, and I felt very loyal to her. But she never appreciated it!"

He sounded pretty cheerful about this, all things considered. As if the years made everything funny to look back on. "Once, she wanted to explore this abandoned building. It wasn't a good idea—the whole thing was falling apart. But your aunt wanted to go, so we went. We split up once we got inside. We were supposed to be looking for something . . . I can't remember what. Something with historical significance—you know your aunt. Anyway, off she went in one direction and me in the other. I was only, what, six or seven? I stepped someplace I shouldn't have and my leg went right through the second floor. I was too scared to move—what if I broke the floor even more and fell all the way down?"

"Did Aunt Lin save you?"

It was strange to hear about Aunt Lin like this—from someone who'd known her the way Mia knew Jake. Mia's mom was Aunt Lin's younger sibling too, but there was such a big age gap between them that Mia often couldn't relate to the way they'd viewed each other, especially when they'd been younger. Things were different now, of course, but once upon a time, Aunt Lin seemed like she'd been half older sister, half second mother to Mia's mom.

"Eventually, she did." He shook his head. "But it took her half an hour. She'd gotten distracted by something or other and had left the house entirely—went so far she couldn't hear me calling for her. By the time she realized she should come looking for me, I'd shouted myself hoarse."

"And then what?" Mia said.

"And then she grabbed my arms and yanked me free, and I had to hide the bruises on my legs for weeks."

"Were you mad at her?"

"For a little while. I was too young to hold a grudge very long, though." He laughed. "These are the things brothers and sisters do to each other, Mia. Don't you agree?"

"I guess."

They'd nearly climbed to their landing, their footfalls echoing through the stairwell. Everything was lit with a pale, diffuse light.

Her uncle already had his key in the lock when he said suddenly, "You know, I have pictures of the Black Pagoda, if you'd like to see them. Old ones, from when I was a child."

"Sure," Mia said, still distracted by his story and then by the look on Jake's face when they entered the apartment—the way he stared at her, accusing and angry for a second, then glancing away again, as if he didn't care at all.

Whatever distance had grown between them the past year, Jake was still her brother; Mia knew when she'd upset him, however much he tried to hide it. Sometimes, in vindictive moments, that knowing was a vicious victory. Right now it just made Mia's chest tighten.

I didn't do anything to him, she told herself. *He's the one who's been ignoring me—who abandoned our treasure hunt.*

But the guilt wouldn't let up. She was almost relieved when he stuck his head into her room later that night and said, his voice low, "You know, Mom would kill me if you got kidnapped in China."

"Only in China?" Mia said, a halfhearted joke that made neither of them laugh. She'd been fiddling with the firework her uncle had bought her, but she set it aside on the bedspread. "I was fine. I didn't get kidnapped. Uncle knew where I was."

"He *guessed* where you *might* be," Jake said, angry and showing it. "Mia, you can't just—"

Mia didn't hear the rest of his words, because she'd heard words like them so many times already that her ears closed when she felt them coming. She didn't need to hear them. She could recite them. She'd been told the same things her whole life—from her mother, from teachers, from *everyone*.

Mia, you can't just get caught up in your own imagination.

Mia, you can't just make things up and say them like they're the truth.

Mia, you can't just ignore the real world.

Mia, come back down to earth.

"Mia—" Jake said, and however sheepish Mia had felt before, it wasn't as furious as she felt now.

"I wouldn't have gone by myself," she snapped, "if you hadn't abandoned everything."

If you'd just believed me about seeing Ying. If you didn't care more about playing basketball with those boys you don't even know—won't ever see again after we go home.

Jake rolled his eyes. "You're always so dramatic."

"Aunt Lin's been *taken*, Jake. And every day we don't solve this is another day that man's got her—I don't know—*tied up* somewhere."

He didn't look at her, but at the door, when he spoke.

"Maybe he doesn't have her, Mia. Maybe she's just off visiting friends, like her letter says."

Mia stared at him, numb, until he finally met her eyes again.

"Fine," she said. "Fine. Then just leave me alone."

He didn't. He opened his mouth to speak, and she jumped off the bed to drive him back out into the hallway. To shut the door in his face.

"That's really mature, Mia," Jake shouted at her through the door. He said it in English, so their uncle couldn't understand—but there was no way anyone could miss the fact that they were fighting.

Mia reached into her bag, where she'd stored Aunt Lin's severed bracelet. She clutched it in her fist and curled up on the bed, shutting her eyes as tightly as she could.

Come back, she thought.

Come back.

Come back.

Somehow, without meaning to, she fell asleep. Her murky dreams were full of twisted, half-familiar faces, along with bits and pieces of Zhu Yunwen's map. Mia dreamed herself back to the Pottery Pagodas of Yongquan Temple, staring at the tiny, hand-crafted buddhas. They whispered something to her, something she couldn't hear.

When she stepped forward, trying to get closer, she somehow tripped and ended up in Sanfang Qixiang, ankle-deep in the scraggly grass outside the ruins of Zhang Jing's house. *Ying is here*, her dream-self thought. She saw him out of the corner of her eye, but no matter how fast she ran, he was always just ahead of her, always a flutter of black clothing turning the corner or dashing down an alleyway, and Mia kept putting on more and more speed until finally, with a flying tackle, she caught him—

Only it wasn't him. It was Aunt Lin. And they weren't in Sanfang Qixiang anymore, but standing in the giant shadow of the Black Pagoda.

Aunt Lin looked as she always looked, except a little fuzzier around the edges, as dream people do. She wore blue jeans and a slightly too-big blouse, little stud earrings glinting in her ears.

"I can't find you," Mia said. Instead of coming out sad or pleading, the words came out angry and frustrated.

The dream-Aunt Lin didn't reply. She just turned

from Mia to the pagoda. Her lips started to move, but before the sounds could reach Mia's ears, she woke to a knock on her door and her uncle calling her to dinner.

It wasn't until later that night, after a tense meal during which both Mia and Jake studiously deflected their uncle's attempts at conversation, that Mia remembered what her uncle had said about his old photographs of the Black Pagoda. Even then, she only remembered because he'd left the photo album on her desk, spread to the right page.

She quickly found the pictures her uncle had wanted her to see. Like he'd said, he'd only been a little boy in them, chubby-cheeked and squinting into a winter sun. He was so bundled up that he was practically as wide as he was tall.

There were only two snapshots. One of them was wide-angled, with Mia's uncle taking up a tiny portion of the frame. Even so, she could tell he was staring at the camera with a goofy expression, like he was laughing at the photographer. The other one was a close-up, his face looming large next to one of the stone figures at the base of the pagoda.

Mia couldn't help laughing. It looked like he was trying to copy the stone figure's serene expression but couldn't quite hide his grin.

Wait.

Mia lifted the album off the desk. The photograph, like all the others on the page, was black-and-white, but it was clear enough to see *something* etched at the bottom of the buddha's cheek.

She scrambled up from the chair and made a beeline for her uncle. He was out on the balcony, watering his plants, and to his credit, he didn't ask her any delaying questions when she spat out an excited, garbled request for a magnifying glass.

Magnified, the buddha's face looked a little distorted, and a lot grainy, but the scratchy marks to the side of his chin were definitely more than just slips of a stonemason's chisel or faults in the photograph.

They were a pattern.

It was a good thing she'd done this twice already, because as Mia pulled out her map and copied the lines down, she was so shaky she could barely get the pattern right.

Magnifying glass still grasped in her fist, she ran back

out onto the balcony and—and *almost* threw her arms around her uncle to hug him. A bit of her happy delirium cleared at the last minute. She stuttered to a stop, shy and awkward again.

In the end, she just gave him the magnifying glass back and grinned—a big, show-every-tooth sort of grin that only got wider as he grinned confusedly back.

19

THERE WAS ONLY ONE CLUE LEFT. ONE MORE space on the map left blank. It occurred to Mia, as she brushed her teeth the next morning, that even a complete map wasn't much good if she didn't know where to start. She'd spent half the night staring at the patterns she'd already copied onto the page, trying to decipher their meaning.

It looked like abstract art. Something interesting to hang on the wall, maybe, but nothing that represented any place Mia knew of. Would the final piece make everything click together? Or would she just be left with another mystery?

But that was something she could worry about later. For now there was still one more riddle to solve.

> *I lie cloistered in a shadowy mountain glen*
> *Edged by sea, enclosed by sturdy walls of stone*
> *But protection of my eternal sleep*
> *Lies with the twin dragons stretched out below*
> *Approach me at my final rest*
> *And look for me at the head.*

She pondered it all through breakfast. And then all through a long, fancy lunch with yet another group of her mom's old friends, who alternately cooed over Mia and ignored her while she and Jake sat politely and bored stiff in their chairs, eyes wandering from the red-and-gold embroidered tablecloth to the glass lazy Susan laden with food, to the crisp white napkins and shimmery chandelier.

Usually, they could have at least thrown each other secret, exasperated looks when the adults weren't paying attention. But they weren't talking, so they just stewed in their separate boredoms until lunch ended.

Things weren't any better back at the apartment. Even with a fan blowing right at her, Mia felt so riotously hot she thought she might explode. She paced the apartment, muttering the riddle to herself under her breath, until her mom asked her to *please be a little quieter, Mia, so I can take a nap*.

"Where are you going?" her uncle asked when he saw her pulling on her shoes.

"Nowhere," Mia huffed. "Downstairs. Out."

It wasn't any cooler outdoors, but a bit of the jittery energy beneath Mia's skin calmed as she threw herself onto the apartment building's front steps. She tilted her face toward the afternoon sun, her eyes closing—then popping back open as something, *someone*, cast a shadow over her.

It was one of the boys Jake played basketball with. He was dressed for a game, wearing a sleeveless shirt and clunky, purple tennis shoes. He smiled. "Hey, you're Jake's little sister, right? Is he coming down?"

"I don't know." The answer came out pricklier than Mia had intended. How did Jake always find a cheerful word for strangers? "He didn't tell me," she amended, try-ing to make her voice sound the way Jake's did—casual, friendly. "Do you have a game today?"

"Just a practice," he said. "We're playing another team tomorrow, though." Maybe Mia's attempts were working, because instead of walking away, he added, "Jake said you guys were working on a project together. Researching an old emperor—Zhu Yunwen?"

"Something like that," Mia said, startled. She hadn't imagined Jake would tell his new friends anything about their treasure hunt. She wasn't sure if she was pleased that he'd acknowledged it, or betrayed that he'd talked about their secret.

"He's a strange emperor to focus on," the boy said. "He was barely on the throne at all. Is he famous in America?"

Mia squinted against the sun to meet his eyes, trying to decide if he was actually interested, or just being polite. Maybe he was only humoring her until Jake came downstairs. But no, he was waiting patiently for her answer, his eyebrows raised—expectant.

Haltingly, she told him how Zhu Yunwen's story was something she'd shared with her aunt. When it became clear that the boy barely knew anything about the emperor, Mia found herself slipping effortlessly into the story. How Zhu Yunwen had escaped from his uncle's soldiers the night of his supposed assassination. How some people said he'd eventually become a monk, cloistered in an isolated monastery up in the mountains, to better hide himself. And all the while, dreaming, dreaming of the day when he might take power again.

It was easy to keep the conversation going when she

talked about history. Easy to forget to be shy or awkward.

"He died before he could rule again," she said. "They probably buried him as a monk by the monastery—"

She cut off midsentence.

An idea had come to her. An answer to the riddle she'd pondered so long and hard. She only dared to approach it sideways in her mind, as if afraid it would dart off again if it saw her.

It didn't dart off again. Just grew more concrete with every moment.

The apartment door blew open, almost knocking her off the steps. She scrambled out of the way just in time to see Jake skid to a surprised stop. They stared awkwardly at each other, neither speaking.

Then his friend pulled him away. As they walked off, Mia heard him say, laughing, "Your little sister's pretty interesting, isn't she?"

She didn't hear Jake's reply.

After Mia borrowed her mom's laptop to do some searching online, she became more convinced that her initial idea was right. She'd figured out the location of the last clue.

There was only one problem.

Every time Mia and Jake fought, it was like a stony game of Who'll Blink First afterward, waiting to see who'd make the first step toward peace. Back when they were younger, it had almost always been Mia—even when it had been Jake who'd started the fight and said the worst things while they were angry.

She'd always hated it when they weren't speaking with each other. The silence would stretch inside her like razor wire until she couldn't take it any longer.

You have a soft heart, Aunt Lin always said, laughing gently, when Mia gave in. *It's not a bad thing.*

This evening, though, as Mia approached Jake in the hallway, watching him pull off his tennis shoes, she didn't know what she was going to say. She wasn't ready for apologies. Most of the time, she and Jake didn't do apologies anyway. They made up with rolled eyes and only said what was absolutely necessary.

Jake saw her coming and paused in the middle of untying his laces.

"Did your team win?" Mia asked. "The practice game?"

Jake made an affirmative sort of noise.

She hesitated. Reminded herself that he'd cared enough about the treasure hunt to tell his new friends. That had to mean something, right? If he was secretly embarrassed by it, or thought it was childish, he wouldn't have talked about it.

"I've almost finished the map."

Jake lifted an eyebrow. Encouraged by this sign of interest, Mia continued speaking. "There's only one piece missing, and I've already solved the riddle—it's Zhu Yunwen's grave."

"His grave?" Jake frowned. "How're we supposed to know where that is? I thought he ran off and died as a nobody somewhere."

Mia shoved an article into his hands. She'd printed it out from her uncle's computer.

"You know I can't read this—" Jake started to say, and exasperated, Mia pointed to the picture of a small, stone pedestal toward the top of the article. An oblong, tombstone-like object sat atop it.

"People discovered this a while back, up in the mountains. They used to think it was only a monk's grave, but that never really made sense, because of decorations around the tombstone. There are dragons, and dragons are an emperor's symbol—back then you couldn't just use them for anyone. And the location makes sense, Jake. It matches the poem. It's by the coast, so there's water, and it's up in the mountains—it's the place the riddle's talking about. I'm sure of it."

She paused as their mother came into the living room, chatting with their uncle. Neither seemed to have heard anything. After a moment she turned back to her brother.

He hesitated, still crouched on the ground, one shoe untied. "Is it close by?"

"I've looked it up," she whispered. "It's too far to take buses, but if we take a train, it'll only be about forty minutes—we can be there and back before anyone misses us."

"Forty minutes by *train*? That's not anywhere near the city, Mia."

She pressed her lips together, then admitted, "It's in Ningde. It's another city, kinda northeast of Fuzhou. Forty minutes isn't a lot of time, Jake—"

"But it's far," he said. "And that's not counting how long it'll take to get to the station here, or from the station in Ningde to the grave site. If it's really up in the mountains, then it's probably not anywhere near the city. We'll have to take a bus—if there's even a bus. We don't know anything about Ningde, Mia."

Mia hadn't thought about those things. Not in any amount of detail anyway. They hadn't mattered. The only thing she'd cared about was getting to Ningde—getting to Zhu Yunwen's grave. Solving the map. Finding the treasure. Saving Aunt Lin.

Everything else seemed trivial in comparison. Doable, as long as she kept her eye on the goal.

"I can figure all that out. I have the train schedule for tomorrow—"

"*Tomorrow?* No way you're going tomorrow, Mia."

"I didn't mean by myself," she said softly. "I thought maybe you'd want to come too."

He was quiet again for several long seconds.

"I know you don't believe Aunt Lin's been taken," Mia mumbled, "but the map's still real."

Slowly, he stood. "I'm not saying I won't go. I just can't go *tomorrow*, okay? I've got a game, and they'll be a player short without me. I can't abandon them like that."

You're fine with abandoning me, Mia thought. *You're fine with abandoning this treasure hunt—this search for Aunt Lin.*

She'd been stupid to be hopeful. Stupid to think this was nearly as important to him as it was to her, whatever he'd said to his friends.

Jake leaned down and gripped her gently by the shoulders. "You promise you won't go alone?" he said. "You promise you'll wait for me?"

"I promise," Mia said.

Jake stuck out his hand, his face solemn. "Shake on it."

So Mia did.

But she didn't mean it.

20

THE FIRST TRAIN FROM FUZHOU TO NINGDE
left a little after seven thirty a.m. It was, Mia figured, her
best shot if she was going to do this alone. She'd wake
up early and be out of the house before anyone else had
risen. Her mom and uncle would notice when she didn't
come for breakfast, of course, but they'd go to Jake first,
and he'd know where she'd gone.

Besides, her mom might not even wake up until mid-
morning. It was nearly midnight, and Mia could still hear
her through the apartment's thin walls, pacing her bedroom
and doing her Polite but Upset voice on the phone. Another
business call had come in after dinner, pulling her mom out
of the bathroom before she'd even had time to rinse the

toothpaste from her mouth. She'd been shut away ever since. From the way the muffled conversation seemed to be going, Mia wouldn't be surprised if things lasted until dawn.

It sucked that her family would worry, but that was unavoidable.

Mia had to do this. Even if they didn't understand.

She laid out everything she'd need—a few bills, filched from her mother's purse, her messenger bag, the now-ragged copy of Zhu Yunwen's map. Then she set her watch alarm for six a.m. and lay tossing and turning in bed until she fell into an uneasy sleep.

The alarm shocked her into fretful wakefulness and the pale morning light. She stumbled out of bed and into her clothing, reaching last for the messenger bag, which she slung across her chest. It seemed heavier than usual. She went over the items inside, picturing each in her head: the compass Thea had given her, the box of matches, the sewing kit—

Oh, and the firework her uncle had bought for her. That was why the bag felt heavier.

She started to take it out, then changed her mind. It didn't add all *that* much weight, and it was actually sort of nice, having something from him to carry with her.

She tied the bright strands of Aunt Lin's bracelet, heavily frayed now, to her bag's strap. And then she was ready.

Or almost ready.

Her gaze fell on Aunt Lin's notebook, lying crooked on the desk. She hesitated. Maybe she ought to leave a note. Even if Jake could tell her mom and uncle everything, maybe it would be better if they had something in Mia's own words too.

She sat at the desk, pen against the page, imagining her mother finding this in a few hours when she came to check on Mia and no one answered her knock. Imagining what she might tell her so she'd worry less—so she wouldn't be angry. What she could write to Jake to explain why she'd had to break her promise to him.

Nothing came.

She sat there and sat there as the pen pressed harder against the page, leaving a dark splotch of ink.

After an eon, she set the pen down.

She couldn't do it. There was nothing to say to her mom, or to Jake, or even to her uncle—who was no longer a stranger, not anymore. Because she couldn't just leave them. Not like this.

She shoved the notebook away and leaned back, defeated, in her chair. She'd have to wait for Jake to come with her. Then, at least, their mom wouldn't worry—not if she thought they were close by and they returned before nightfall.

A knock sounded at the door, surprising her so badly she nearly tipped over in the chair.

It must be Mom, she thought. But when she opened the door, it was Jake.

He'd obviously just gotten up—his hair stuck up in all directions, and he was still wearing his pajamas. Even as she stared at him, he yawned so wide she thought he might crack his jaw. But he didn't seem surprised to find her dressed and ready to go.

"We should stay for breakfast, at least," he said as she gaped at him. He smiled, just a little. "Then we can go catch that train."

The train station was a crush of people. Mia and Jake kept tight hold of each other as they pushed through the crowds. Neither of them made even a perfunctory grumble about having to hold the other's hand. If they got separated here, they'd never find each other again.

The train itself was only slightly less crowded. An eclectic collection of people shuffled through the corridors, finding their seats. The briefcase carriers and high-heel wearers intermingled with women carrying baskets full of fresh fruit or spotted brown eggs. A little girl ran laughing up and down the aisles in a pink princess dress, grinning at Mia every time she passed.

Then came a warning beep on the overhead speakers, and the train lurched from the station. They were off.

It wasn't the first time Mia had taken a train in China. She'd sat between Aunt Lin and Jake during the long ride from Shanghai to Fuzhou. But she'd been exhausted then, fresh off a fifteen-hour flight and still smelling of stale airplane air. She'd spent most of the ride asleep, her head lolling against Aunt Lin's shoulder.

This time, she'd nabbed a window seat. The landscape flashed by, at first nothing interesting—just a series of tunnels—then widening and unfurling into rolling greenery as they left Fuzhou behind. Mountains rose around them, lush under an achingly blue sky. When the lakes came, they were just as blue, as if two polished mirrors sandwiched the world between them: the mountains, the train tracks, the train, Mia.

By the time they arrived at the Ningde station, it felt like they'd traveled a lot more than forty minutes away—even if it was forty minutes by high-speed train. Mia realized suddenly, as she stepped onto the platform, how far she and Jake were from the apartment in Fuzhou. From their mom and uncle, who thought they were just visiting another tourist site around the city center.

"What're you staring at?" Jake said as he strode past her. He paused when she didn't answer, giving her a questioning look over his shoulder.

Mia gripped the strap of her messenger bag. "Nothing," she said. "Let's go."

Unofficial taxi drivers milled around the train station. They weren't like the taxis Mia saw on television, bright yellow and clearly marked with a sign on the roof. These just looked like normal cars, their drivers rolling down their windows and calling out to passersby, asking if they wanted a ride.

They found one willing to take them to Zhu Yunwen's grave site, then bartered the price down to something reasonable. Mia wasn't used to arguing about prices, but they didn't have a lot of money left, so now seemed like a good time to give it a go. The driver stared at her, amused, the whole time.

"So, why're you two so interested in Zhu Yunwen's grave?" he said once they were in his car, swinging around the looping mountain roads.

"I like history," Mia said simply.

He laughed. "And your parents? They don't like history?"

"They're busy today," Jake said quickly before Mia could reply. "They're just staying in the city." He tapped at the car window, gesturing to the swatches of carefully pruned plants flying past. "What're they growing there?"

"Tea leaves," the driver said, latching happily on to the new topic. "One of Ningde's specialties."

The rest of the ride passed quickly, full of dangerously tight turns and his cheerful chatter about tea. Mia twisted Aunt Lin's bracelet in her hands.

Soon they were wending beneath a thick canopy of lanky trees, the sun a scattering of fractured yellow light. The driver pulled into a small parking lot and smiled at them through the rearview mirror. "Well, here you are: history."

Jake looked like he was trying not to roll his eyes. He

ushered Mia out of the taxi and reached into his pocket for their money.

"Where is it?" Mia said, looking around. "The grave?"

The driver rolled down his window. "Up there—follow the path. It isn't far."

The woods were peaceful, devoid of people except for Mia and Jake. Devoid of sound, even, but for the whisper of wind through trees and the occasional song from a faraway bird. Everything was green, green, green, spindly trees and tufts of tall grass erupting from every inch of unpaved road.

It was a far cry from the chaos of the train station. Here, it was like they were alone in the world. It was that feeling, perhaps, that gave Mia the gumption to say, a little shyly, "Thanks for changing your mind, Jake."

What she meant was, *Thanks for coming with me*, but she couldn't quite manage to say it. Besides, Jake understood.

"Is your team mad?" she added quickly. "About you leaving them a player short?"

He shrugged and smiled at her. "Maybe I'll still make it, if we get back early. If not—well, I told them my family had something important going on. One of them's got a friend who can sub in for me."

Without warning, the path delivered them to an opening in the woods—a series of raised stone daises tucked into a semicircle niche among the trees. At the topmost dais, ensconced within a wide loop of thick, stone wall, was the pedestal and tombstone Mia had seen online.

A shivery feeling danced across Mia's skin. Here lay the man who'd started everything more than five hundred years ago. He'd been dead about that long too. Yet the ripples of his dreams still rocked her life today.

Would she, Mia Chen, dream anything that big? Do anything that significant?

If she did, would she know about it?

She climbed the stone-cut stairs to the second dais. Twin dragons stretched on either side of the tombstone, just like the article had said. Unlike the other dragons decorating shops and temples Mia had seen since her arrival, these were only vaguely dragonlike. Their bodies were thin and rod-straight, their mouths open in a strange grimace. The designs down their necks, rippling in an imagined wind, seemed more like leaves or ribbons than proper scales.

Mia ran a hand over one of their sun-warmed snouts. Strange dragons for a strange emperor. Who had buried him here and tried to give him a ruler's send-off despite his anonymous death? Had they known about his hidden treasure?

They must have, to have instructed someone to hide a clue on his tombstone.

"Look, someone's left a clementine for him." Mia approached the altarlike pedestal supporting the tombstone. She reached out to touch the fruit, then decided against it at the last moment. She wasn't sure if there were rules about things like that, and the last thing she needed was to offend the very man whose treasure she was after.

"Come on, Jake," she said, reaching for their copy of the map. She couldn't hear his footsteps, despite the near silence of the woods. "You think we should start looking on the tombstone itself, or everywhere around the grave? The riddle wasn't very specific. . . ."

He didn't reply.

"Jake?"

She turned, frowning—and froze.

Jake lay crumpled at the bottom of the stairs.

He fell, she thought. *He fell and hit his head and—*

A second figure emerged from behind the swell of the

wall. A tall man with a cloud of black hair who walked, then ran toward her. Who grabbed her—frozen where she stood—and stuffed a foul-smelling rag against her nose and mouth.

Mia screamed into it. She screamed and screamed, but no sound escaped.

A thick, muddy fist closed around her mind.

Her legs gave out first.

She was unconscious before she hit the ground.

21

WAKING WAS LIKE CLAWING UP FROM THE
bottom of a deep, cold well. Even after her eyes opened,
Mia's thoughts weren't entirely there, parts of her slower
than others to get their affairs straight.

She heard a whisper: "Mia?"

Her name traveled like an electric spark down her
spine, jolting everything to life. Because the voice that
spoke it—that familiar, much-loved voice—belonged to
someone she'd half feared she might never see again.

"Aunt Lin!" she cried hoarsely. Wherever she was, it
was pitch-black. Mia could hardly see her own hands, let
alone anyone else. "Where's Jake? Is he here?"

"He's right beside you," Aunt Lin said. "Don't worry. He'll be all right."

Mia tried to stand, and quickly discovered two things. One, her hands were bound in front of her by something harsh and plasticky. Two, her legs weren't as stable as she'd thought. She tumbled down again, banging her shin against something in the darkness.

"Hold on, hold on," Aunt Lin said. There was a rattling sound. Then a weak glow flickered to life in her hands, powered by a tiny, plastic flashlight, like the kind you'd find on a key chain. Her wrists were bound, too. She had to fiddle with the flashlight to get it pointed where she wanted.

She swept the light around them, revealing the cramped insides of a van. Men's clothing hung haphazardly from the seats. Empty and half-empty food containers scattered about the floor, now and then abutting against a plastic water bottle. It all smelled too—sour and too sweet and musty.

Jake slumped against one of the lumpy seats, still unconscious. A nasty bruise marred his temple, where he must have hit the ground, but he seemed to be breathing okay. Mia fought the urge to shake him awake, to make sure.

"I found the flashlight in this mess," Aunt Lin said, gesturing around them. "But the battery's running out, so we shouldn't waste it."

"Are you okay?" Mia folded herself against Aunt Lin. "Did he hurt you?"

Aunt Lin gave a little laugh. It didn't sound completely real, but it made Mia feel a tiny bit better anyway. "I'm fine, darling. Your aunt is pretty sturdy, don't you think? How are your mother and uncle—were they with you? Do they know you're missing?"

"I don't know," Mia said. "They're still in Fuzhou. Jake and I came to the grave alone. They all thought you'd just left—they believed that letter. But I didn't."

Aunt Lin kissed the top of her head. She looked like she'd spent the past days in the same clothing, the blouse wrinkled, her hair wispy around her face in untamed curls. But her smile was steady. "I didn't think you would. Everything is going to be okay, Mia."

She sounded so sure that Mia found it easy to be sure as well. But that lasted only a moment. Her eyes landed on Jake again, on his bruised temple, and her chest tightened.

She climbed over to the van's door and rattled it, trying to slide it open. It didn't give.

"Where are we?" she said. "Where's Ying?"

Aunt Lin shook her head. "I don't know. He barely lets me out of this van—he's afraid I'll call for help. He's been driving me all over—"

"Trying to solve the riddles, right?" Mia said. Automatically, she tried to reach for her messenger bag. "That's what Jake and I were doing too. That's why we were at Zhu Yunwen's grave. We almost had it finished—"

Aunt Lin's mouth formed a hard line. "Ying did too. He might have the whole thing now. The grave site was his last riddle."

A squealing noise put a halt to their conversation. Aunt Lin extinguished her flashlight just in time. A second later the rusty van door wrenched open. Ying loomed in the scant opening.

At first he was little more than a dark shape haloed by sunlight. Mia blinked rapidly, willing her eyes to readjust. Then flinched as he tossed something at her—a crumpled-up sheet of blue notebook paper.

"What does it mean?" he growled.

Jake groaned and shifted, prodded awake by his voice. Ying ignored him, gesturing wildly for Mia to pick up the fallen ball of paper. He didn't look well. His hair was an uncombed thatch, his skin pale and drawn, as if he hadn't slept in days. He smelled of sour desperation and anger.

Mia kept her head down as she reached for the paper. It wasn't easy. Her wrists chaffed painfully against their plastic ties. Aunt Lin went to Jake, whispering for him to stay calm as he came to.

"What does what mean?" Mia willed her voice steady as she smoothed out the paper. The lines on it were a little different from the ones she was used to—drawn by a different hand—but the overall effect was the same. It was Zhu Yunwen's map, completed.

How strange to hold it in her hands. She noticed that three of the patterns, fitted together like this, lead the eye toward one particular spot on the map—a place where the lines congregated to form something circular.

"The map." Even angry and frustrated, there was a dark control about Ying, like a black cloak. All his feelings seemed to turn inward. "It's finished, isn't it? But it doesn't tell me where to go. It's not a map of China. It's not a map of Fujian Province. It's not a map of anything!"

Jake was all the way awake now. He met eyes with

Mia, the two of them exchanging a loaded look. *We have to keep him calm*, it said. *We have to buy time.*

Time for what? Not for rescue—no one knew where they were.

An escape, then.

"She doesn't know what it means, Ying," Aunt Lin said softly. "She's only a little girl."

Ying pulled a terrible scowl. "She figured everything else out, didn't she?" He swung to face Mia. "Did someone help you? Was it your mother?"

"*No*," Mia said, terrified. Would he go after her mom next? "No one helped me."

"Well," Ying said, "then you can figure this out too."

He grabbed the van door and pulled it shut again.

22

MIA WASN'T SURE HOW YING EXPECTED THEM
to work on anything in the darkness. But the man hadn't
looked like he was thinking clearly. That could be a plus.
The more frazzled and sleep-deprived he was, the easier
it would be to escape.

At least, Mia hoped so. Because it also made him
more frightening—more uncontrolled. Like he might do
anything and everything to get what he wanted.

Aunt Lin turned on the flashlight again, giving them
the small comfort of its glow. Mia still felt a shot of relief
every time she saw her aunt's face. But there wasn't time
to celebrate.

"I think we're still out in the countryside," Jake said,

shoving himself upright. He pressed his clenched fists against his head, like he was nursing a powerful headache. "I looked past him while you guys were talking. There were mountains and a lot of trees."

"We must be near a village, though," Aunt Lin said. "We've been here a night already, and he brought back food once—and it wasn't packaged like it would be from a larger town or from the city."

Mia bit her lip. "So if we got out of the van and ran, we could find it?"

She didn't like to imagine what would happen if they didn't. If they simply got lost in the wilderness, wandering about the mountainside in circles until they collapsed from exhaustion and thirst.

"We'd have to get out of the van first," Aunt Lin said.

"We could overpower him," Jake said. "There are three of us and only one of him. He doesn't look that steady on his feet."

Aunt Lin lifted her hands, the plastic zip ties glinting in the flashlight's glow. "These need to come off first."

Mia noticed, with an uneasy churn of her stomach, that her aunt's wrists were the same molted, bruised color as Jake's temple. How long had she been tied up like this? Mia didn't like to think about it.

"Wait," she said. The idea, when it came, struck her like a train. She scrambled for her messenger bag, yanking it open. It was three times as hard as usual, with her bound hands, but she finally managed to find what she was looking for—her sewing kit. She pried the case open and finagled out a pair of tiny silver scissors. They were barely longer than her thumb and rounded at the tips—airport-security safe.

But they were also sharp as anything along the blade. Sharp enough, certainly, to cut through plastic zip ties.

"You are a marvel," Aunt Lin said, when she saw the scissors in Mia's hands. Despite everything, Mia smiled, just a little.

They maneuvered so Mia could saw through the plastic around Aunt Lin's wrists. Then Aunt Lin freed her and Jake. They sat for a moment, rubbing their wrists. Jake nursed his head.

Mia hesitated, then added, "Should we try to run at night? So he can't follow us so easily?"

"We can't see either, at night." Jake winced as he spoke, squeezing his eyes shut.

"You need to rest before we do anything," Aunt Lin told him. "By the time you're ready to move, it'll probably be near dark anyhow. Running at night might not be a bad idea. We just need to get away from the van. Then we can hide somewhere until morning, if we need to."

A moment passed, tense and unhappy, while they pondered this plan. It wasn't perfect, but it was the only one they had.

"Here," Aunt Lin said. She grabbed some bottles of water, then fished around until she found a half-empty box of crackers. "Eat and drink and put some in that bag of yours. When we're ready, we'll call for him, tell him we have an idea about the map. Then we'll knock him unconscious and run."

Jake picked up a metal tea canteen rolling about his feet. He nodded, his face steely.

Aunt Lin slumped again. Mia was reminded, suddenly, that Ying had once been a good friend of her aunt's. That this search for Zhu Yunwen's treasure had been a shared dream of theirs, pursued by lamplight after long days in the fields.

The van filled with a hot, tense silence.

"I hoped I could reason with him," Aunt Lin said

finally, quietly. "He wants the money for his wife. He just wants to make the rest of her life a little easier. I keep telling him there are other ways, that she wouldn't want this. But he's always been stubborn."

She leaned her head against one of the battered seats while Mia forced herself to nibble on a cracker. It was hard to swallow, but the thought of starving out there on the mountainside made her keep at it. After a moment, Jake sidled up next to her, the metal canteen still clutched in his fist.

Mia had dreamed, for years, of Zhu Yunwen's treasure.

She'd dreamed, for years, of adventure. Of danger and mortal peril and finding her way home again by the skin of her teeth.

She'd never realized until now how important that last bit was. How horrific an adventure could turn out if there was no grand victory at the end of it.

But she kept her fears to herself. She could tell her aunt was frightened and worried—and Jake, too, for all he tried to keep stoic. It wouldn't help anything to cry or make a fuss.

So Mia sat there in the darkness, nibbling at crackers and taking sips of water while Jake recovered a little from his blow to the head. While they all gathered their strength.

Every once in a while, she'd press the back of her hand against the van windows. They'd been covered up from the outside, but she could still feel the heat of the sun on them—and the way they cooled as the evening wore on.

The windowpane grew cold. Jake's gaze steadied.

"Ready?" Aunt Lin whispered.

Mia nodded.

Mia was closest to the van's sliding door, so she was the one to kick her foot against it, yelling, "Hello? Hello? I think I've figured it out. *Hello?*"

There was no answer, and Mia feared that Ying had left them. Maybe just to get food. Maybe forever.

What if he'd tired of waiting for them to come up with an answer, or had decided that they were more trouble than they were worth? What if he'd already figured out the map himself, and was off with the treasure, leaving the three of them stuck here in the dark?

Shaking a little, she kicked harder. *"Hello? Hello?"*

The door popped open. Mia jerked backward just in

time to keep from tumbling into Ying. He scowled down at her—but she saw the glint of hope in his eyes. Just for a second.

Then Jake swooped from his hiding place at the edge of the doorway. The canteen glinted in a shaft of moonlight—then smashed down on the side of Ying's head. He staggered, bellowing in pain.

"Go! Go!" Aunt Lin cried.

Mia's arms and legs felt like tangled string. She couldn't find her balance. Jake leaped from the van. He reached back for her, waving her toward him, and she tried to put her feet in the right order—to run. Somehow, without knowing how it happened, she was on the ground—was on her feet—was darting with Jake away from the van.

But Aunt Lin was slower. She tripped on her way out. She fell.

Ying grabbed at her and caught her arm.

Aunt Lin stared straight at Mia. "Go!" she shouted.

But Mia couldn't leave her.

She skidded to a stop and ran back, ignoring Jake's cry of protest. Ying dragged Aunt Lin back toward the van door. He bled from his temple where Jake had struck

him, and there was a horrific expression on his face—
fear and anger and desperation all rolled into one.

Mia slammed into him, pushing and kicking. She'd
never fought anyone before—not for real, not with
deadly intent, like she did now.

Let her go! she screamed in her head. She was too
breathless, her lungs too tight, to do so aloud. *Let her
go—let her go—*

With a grunt of pain, Ying did. Mia had managed
a powerful kick to his knee, toppling him sideways—
and bringing her down with him. They tumbled to the
ground, tangled together like a lion and its fallen prey.
Who was lion and who was prey, Mia wasn't sure.

All she knew was that she needed to get up again,
because Aunt Lin was free and they needed to run.

She limped to her feet—and fell again when Ying's
fingers closed around her ankle. She twisted, jabbing at
him with her other foot, wishing she were wearing steel-
toed boots instead of her soft running shoes. But it was
enough. He released her.

She grabbed Aunt Lin's hand. Yanked her toward
Jake, who'd come back to try to help.

They ran, blindly, into the darkness.

23

THEY HAD BOTH THE BLESSING AND THE CURSE
of a full moon. A blessing because it lit the rocky terrain around them—pale, white light slipping through the shifting canopy of trees. A curse because it meant Ying could see his way, too. Mia heard him blasting through the woods behind them.

It was impossible to move quietly through the underbrush. Every step betrayed them. But they couldn't stop moving, either. So they ran and ran. Mia thought they might be headed downhill, but it was hard to tell. The land sloped every which way.

Then it fell away altogether.

Jake nearly fell off the edge. He windmilled backward.

They'd come upon a cliff.

Jake approached the edge again, more carefully this time, and peered over the side. He shook his head, whispering, "It's too steep. We'll have to go another way."

Aunt Lin was already turning to go. For the moment the woods were quiet. Ying was probably waiting, listening to hear their direction. Mia flushed with adrenaline, but her legs were starting to go numb and her chest hurt. Aunt Lin seemed even worse off, her breaths coming in little gasps.

How much longer could they run?

"Come on, Mia." Aunt Lin pulled at Mia's hand.

But Mia hesitated. She'd been staring at the landscape beyond the edge of the cliff as she pondered things, and now, just as she thought about leaving, she realized she didn't want to. Something about that land called to her. Was familiar to her.

She disentangled herself from Aunt Lin's hand and walked to the edge of the cliff, staring hard at the swoop of the mountains, the way a small, lithe river reflected moonlight as it slithered down the slopes.

All at once, two things came to her:

The first was that this was the land in the painting.

There loomed the mountains behind the two dancing cranes. They rose black beneath the moonlight—their rough shapes drawn out as if by the strokes of an inky paintbrush.

The second hit her like a stroke of fire, burning up her insides—

The lines of the landscape matched the lines of Zhu Yunwen's map.

"It's here," she breathed.

"What?" Aunt Lin took Mia's hand again. "Darling, we have to go. Now."

"It's here." Mia's discovery was so big, so all-encompassing, that it was hard to speak. "The map. Zhu Yunwen's map—it's here. The lines—see? The river over there and these rows of rocks. And the mountains in the background. They fit with the lines in the map!"

Jake hurried up beside her, and Aunt Lin squeezed between them, all three of them taking in the moon-drenched mountainside.

"I think she's right," Jake whispered.

Mia chose not to be offended by the surprise in his voice. There wasn't time. A crack came from the darkness—the crunch of someone moving toward them.

They had only a few moments before Ying caught up. Mia searched the landscape one last time, looking for that spot she remembered—the one toward the center of the map, where three patterns came together to form a circle. She thought she saw it in a swirl of stone boulders by the side of the mountain wall below. There wasn't time to make sure.

"We have to find a way down," she said.

"Mia," Aunt Lin said, "we can look for the treasure later—"

Mia shook her head. "No, no—we can hide there. Wherever the treasure is!"

Wherever Zhu Yunwen had hidden his treasure all these years—it had to be a good enough hiding place for the three of them now.

They tripped along, picking their way downhill and trying not to fall. Mia kept a tight grip on her aunt's hand, so they could catch each other if one lost her balance. She'd never done anything like this in the dark before, but she'd gone hiking often enough back home. She knew how to angle her feet so they wouldn't slip, how to test for steady ground that wouldn't roll or crumble beneath her weight.

Still, they slid more than walked the last few yards down the cliffside, their faces and hands scratched from shoving through the underbrush. Mia was the smallest, so she moved quickest through the tangle of trees. She darted ahead from time to time, making sure they were going the right way.

Up close, the boulders were far bigger than they'd looked from the cliff, jutting from the ground like giant, hunchbacked sentinels. The moonlight made them glow pale white. Mia moved from stone to stone—each was nearly as tall as her apartment building back in Fuzhou.

"I think we've lost Ying," Aunt Lin said. She squinted back the way they'd come.

Mia tilted her head and listened hard, but heard nothing more than the chirrup of nighttime insects, interrupted twice by the low bellow of a frog.

Jake joined Mia in her inspection of the great white boulders. They didn't need to speak to know what they were searching for: a pattern like the ones they'd found while putting together the treasure map—a symbol letting them know what to do next.

Please let this be the spot, Mia thought, over and over again. *Please let this be the spot. Please let this be the spot.*

The moon was spotlight bright overhead, the night cloudless. Mia's hands darted over every inch of the stones she could reach, looking for something, anything.

Her fingers brushed against something that wasn't stone. Or stone that didn't feel like normal stone, anyway—stone that had been polished smooth. It was half hidden beneath what seemed like years, maybe decades or even centuries, of dust and mud. Mia rubbed it clean with a bit of her shirt.

"Aunt Lin," she called quietly, beckoning her closer. "Do you still have the flashlight?"

Her aunt did. The light flickered on and off for a few seconds before settling into a weak glow. It was just enough to see what Mia had found: a smooth bit of stone about the size of a man's palm. One edge of it folded inward, forming a crevasse deep enough to fit Mia's entire hand.

She stuck it inside, all the way up to her wrist, not quite sure what she expected to happen. Nothing did.

She tried yanking at the stone, then pushing it. Jake joined her, the two of them straining against the boulder. A shower of dust fell on Mia's head, making her cough. But it was a sign, at least, that they were making progress.

Aunt Lin squeezed her hands in on top of theirs. On Mia's "One, two, three!" they all heaved together, throwing their weight backward, pulling so hard that Aunt Lin's arms trembled and Jake's knuckles shone white and Mia thought her shoulders might pop right out of their sockets.

The stone groaned and shifted, and shifted some more.

A passageway yawned open behind it. A set of stairs descended into the bowels of the earth.

24

A TORCH HUNG ON THE STONE WALL ONLY A
few steps from the entrance. Seeing it gave Mia the same
shivery feeling she'd felt at the foot of Zhu Yunwen's
grave. Someone had left that torch here for her—or
someone like her—to find.

Jake slipped the torch free of its metal rack. He
wrinkled his nose. "Some batteries for the flashlight
might have been more useful."

Wordlessly, Mia reached into her messenger bag and
drew out her box of matches.

The farther underground they ventured, the colder
it grew. The torch's dancing flame cast shadowy twins
of Mia, and Jake, and Aunt Lin, as if they shared this

journey with ghostly versions of themselves. Maybe it was only Mia's imagination, but the air did feel thick with ghosts, or spirits, or *something*.

Jake and Aunt Lin walked gingerly, as if they felt it too.

They came to the end of the stairs. Jake, lighting the way, was about to continue down the tunnel when Mia stopped him with a hushed, *"Wait*—there's someone there, up ahead."

Was it Ying, waiting for them in the shadows? Had he somehow made it to the treasure site ahead of them? Was there some other way in?

They waited, breath held. The figure, whoever it was, didn't seem to have heard them. It didn't seem to see their light either. In fact, it didn't move at all—not even the natural shuffling and fidgeting of any person who'd stood in place too long.

"Stay here," Mia whispered. Before anyone could stop her, she tiptoed to get a closer look.

The figure stayed frozen as she approached. Mia's heart pounded, and she had to force herself forward the last few steps, stopping just out of arm's reach.

She sighed in relief. It was only a statue.

Preserved here, in the cool darkness beneath the

mountain, the figure seemed untouched by time. Mia made out the neat lines of his face, the carefully carved flow of his beard. The man was almost life-size—a good head or two taller than Mia. He stared blankly at the tunnel wall across from him, his expression a contemplative frown.

"Do you think it's him?" she said as Aunt Lin drew up next to her and Jake brought the torch. "Zhu Yunwen?"

For a long moment, Aunt Lin seemed too overwhelmed to speak. She looked at the statue, then at the stairs they'd just descended, and then at the tunnel that still stretched before them. Her hands shook a little. Mia took one and squeezed it in comfort.

"I think it could be," Aunt Lin said.

They moved onward, silence-bound. The history of the place hung around them like invisible cobwebs.

Abruptly, the tunnel turned a corner and ended, broadening into a room. And in the room, lit by the flame of their torch, lay an immensity of wealth like nothing Mia had ever seen before.

Golden necklaces piled on silver statuettes, their sinuous lengths embedded with precious jewels. Delicate jade sculptures of birds and beasts swam among strands of snowy pearls. Two golden dragons curled toward each other atop an ornate lacquered chest, clutching between them an enormous bloodred jewel.

Aunt Lin walked like a dreamer from one bit of the treasure trove to another. Her hands flitted toward a vase—a necklace—a statuette, never touching, just feeling at the air around it. A peal of laughter burst from her chest, ringing all the way up to the high ceilings.

"It's real," Jake said to himself, his voice hushed with awe. "It's actually real." He opened one of the chests and found it full of golden coins, each with a square hole stamped out of the center.

Marble columns stood at the edges of the room—which was truly a room, with a tiled floor and everything, not just barren rock wall. Even though Mia had been searching so hard for this—had hoped and hoped as she walked along the tunnel—coming across it so suddenly was like stumbling into an oasis after days in the desert.

She stayed by the threshold, giving herself a moment to take it all in.

A cold hand closed around her shoulder. By the time her brain registered the touch—had time to scream *Run, Run!*—it was already too late.

The hand yanked her backward. An arm snaked across her neck, pinning her against a man's chest.

She squirmed and screamed, but it was no use—she only choked herself in his grip.

"Stop." Ying's voice rang out, low and harsh. His hand flashed. Something cold pressed against the side of Mia's throat. A knife. "All of you—*stop.*"

Mia's legs turned to water.

Aunt Lin looked bloodless in the torchlight, her face as pale as the moon. But she swallowed and spoke. "Let her go, Ying. You've found the treasure—here it is. Just let us go. We won't tell anyone. Who would believe us?"

Ying stood silent and still. Or almost still—Mia felt the tiny tremors running through his arm. Whether he shook with excitement, or rage, or just madness, she wasn't sure. She only knew that the knife in his grip shook too. That it was only millimeters from her skin. That one jerk of his hand would send it biting into her neck.

"What did I say?" he snapped when Jake shifted on his feet. His grip tightened around Mia's throat, cutting off her air. "Nobody move."

Jake froze. Ying relaxed his arm just a fraction, and Mia gasped for breath.

"Ying—" Aunt Lin started to say, but he cut her off savagely, yelling for her to shut up.

A moment later, though, he seemed to calm a little. At least, his voice did. The trembling in his arm and hands didn't stop.

"You promise you won't tell anyone?" he said.

Aunt Lin nodded. He looked over at Jake, who warily did the same. Mia could barely move her head. But he didn't seem to be looking for a response from her anyway.

He took a step backward, dragging her with him. Then he reached into his pocket and took out two of the same plastic ties he'd used to bind everyone up back at the van. He tossed them to Jake.

"Tie your aunt to that column," he told Jake. "Put her hands behind her. Hurry up."

25

JAKE HESITATED, LOOKING FROM MIA TO THEIR
aunt. Finally, his eyes shifted to Ying. "Why?" he said.
"What're you going to do?"

Ying took a sharp breath, like he was trying to keep
his temper. "Tie up your aunt," he repeated. "Then yourself. I'll take the girl with me to get my van. Once I
return, I'll release you, and you'll help me load this stuff
into the back—as much as can fit. Then I'll leave."

"And we'll stay here?" Jake said. "You'll leave us alone?"

Ying nodded. "There's a village not too far away. It
won't be hard to find once it's daylight. You'll be fine. But
you have to tie up your aunt."

"It's all right, Jake." Aunt Lin went to the column that

Ying had pointed out and sat at the base of it. Her eyes never left Mia. "Do as he says."

"He can't just take her," Jake protested. His eyes were very wide. His jaw clenched.

"Jake," Aunt Lin said. "Please."

Reluctantly, he came and did as he was told, binding Aunt Lin's hands behind her with the plastic ties.

"Good," Ying said once he was done. He motioned for Jake to move over a few columns. "Now yourself."

"I can't do it," Jake said. "I can't reach."

Ying gave a growl of frustration, but it was obvious that Jake was telling the truth.

"Walk," he said to Mia. He didn't lift the knife from her throat. "Slowly."

Step by cautious step, the two of them moved forward until they reached Jake. Mia saw that her brother was a hairbreadth from jumping at them—however badly that was likely to go. She gave him the tiniest shake of her head.

Jake was athletic and quick, but the man was much bigger and more broadly built. Plus, he had the knife. Mia didn't want to think about the damage that blade could do to Jake with one slice.

"Turn around," Ying told Jake. "Arms backward around the column—just like that. Go on, pull the tie tight." The last bit was directed at Mia.

She thought about faking it, leaving Jake some room to free himself. But Ying kept urging her to pull tighter and tighter, until Mia knew Jake had no hope of escape.

Ying tugged her backward again, edging toward the doorway. Aunt Lin and Jake stared after them, and Mia saw reflected in their faces her own fear, and apprehension, and dread.

She didn't believe what Ying said about letting them go afterward. She wanted to, but she didn't.

Still, there wasn't any choice. He yanked her into the tunnel, then up the stairs and out of the mountain, into the warm, moon-bathed clearing. He'd left the stone door open. He must have exhausted himself against that stone, to move by himself what had taken Mia, Jake, and their aunt to move together.

To Mia's relief, he let the knife drop from her neck, folding the blade away and slipping it into his pocket. He grabbed her wrist, keeping her tethered to him as he strained against the boulder, shoving it back into place.

The monumental task took a while to accomplish. Which meant Mia had time to think.

It was hard. Her thoughts fumbled about in her head. Anytime she started planning a course of action, it got interrupted by the thought of Ying's knife, or the memory of Aunt Lin and Jake bound to their columns, or the thought of what her mother was thinking back at the apartment—she'd be worried out of her mind by now. What would she do if they didn't return tonight? Or tomorrow?

Or ever, at all?

The last thought shuddered through Mia like a storm, sucking all the strength from her limbs. She stumbled. Irritated, Ying wrenched her upright again, but his grip was looser this time. He was more focused on the stone.

Mia's thoughts focused too. She'd jostled her bag as she fell. And she'd remembered, suddenly, what she still kept inside it: matches, her travel sewing kit, the compass Thea had given her—

And a little exploding firework. The one her uncle had bought for her during their nighttime walk. *They shoot right up into the air,* he'd said. So it had to pack quite a punch.

Especially if Mia shot it straight at someone.

She just needed the chance to light it.

But that chance wasn't now. With one final heave, Ying thrust the boulder back into place, sealing off the treasure tomb. Mia had a sudden, horrible thought—was the door airtight? Even if she did manage to knock Ying out with the firework, she wouldn't be able to move that door on her own. If the door was airtight, Aunt Lin and Jake would suffocate inside.

But she couldn't let her thoughts drift that way. It only made her even more wild with worry. She had to think clearly, instead.

"Come on," Ying said, and pulled her back toward the cliff, toward the van.

He held her by only one wrist, all his attention aimed at carving a path forward. Mia worked her bag open with her free hand and felt for the firework. Slipping it out of the bag little by little, she tucked it into the waistband of her jeans, covering it with her shirt. The box of matches was next, fitting neatly into her pocket.

By this point, they'd reached the base of the cliff. Ying still hadn't given her an opening. She couldn't strike a match with only one hand. Even if she managed to yank her hand from his without breaking her wrist, she'd have only a few seconds of freedom. Not nearly enough to do what she needed to do—strike the match, light the firework, aim it.

She needed Ying to release her on his own.

Which meant she needed him to think she was harmless—too distraught and scared to do anything but follow directions.

Mia had never been good at faking emotions she didn't feel. Luckily, she didn't need to fake any of her terror now. She let herself fall, wincing as the rocky ground banged against her knees.

"I can't go so fast," she said. "Please, my arm hurts. And my legs. I think I'm bleeding."

"You're fine," Ying said gruffly.

Mia let herself cry, just a little. She hated to cry—it made her eyes itch and her head pound, and she always felt exhausted afterward. But she needed to play a role. So she took deep, shuddering breaths, and once the tears started, they had a life of their own and didn't want to stop.

Ying ignored her crying as long as she kept walking. If she stopped, he yanked her moving again. So she didn't stop. She trotted obediently behind him, her wrist limp in his grip.

By the time they reached the top of the cliff, Ying was barely holding on to her at all. His thoughts were obviously elsewhere, maybe trying to retrace his steps to his van, maybe trying to figure out which parts of Zhu Yunwen's treasure he ought to carry away first.

Mia was compliant, sniffling.

Patient. Alert.

Watching for the right moment.

It came just as they reached the clearing where Ying had parked his van. He must have been worried he wouldn't find it again after their headlong rush through the woods, because he huffed a breath of relief as he released Mia's wrist to reach for his keys.

Now! Mia thought. Even as she thought it, she was pulling the box of matches from her pocket with one hand and tugging the firework from her waistband with the other. She drew a match free—swiped it against the side of the box—and set the firework's fuse ablaze.

Ying turned at the sound of the match strike, confused. The befuddled look was still on his face as Mia aimed the firework at him, willing the fuse to burn faster—

It exploded from her hands. Ying leaped aside—just missed it as it shot past his ear, screaming into the dark sky, where it burst into a bloom of red sparks.

Mia's throat closed. She'd missed. She'd missed, she'd missed.

Ying lunged for her, fury electric through every line of him. Mia dove out of the way—realized he'd dropped his keys in surprise when he'd dodged her firework. Without thinking, she scooped them up from the dirt.

She darted for the van. It had been her prison before, but now it was her sanctuary—her fortress. She tumbled inside and slammed the door shut. Locked it. Scrambled to the front seats and made sure the driver's and passenger's side doors were locked too.

Outside, Ying pounded against the van window, the force of it so brutal the whole vehicle shook. Mia moved to the back of the van again, trying to put distance between them, trying to find some other way to protect herself—because if Ying kept attacking the window like this, it would crack, it would break, and then what would she do?

She'd figure out something. *It will be all right*, she told herself as she huddled between the backseats. She raised her arms to shield her head as Ying threw himself at the van again.

It will be all right.

It will be all right.

But what if it wasn't? What if she never saw Jake and Aunt Lin again? Never went home to her mother again? She pressed even harder against the floor—yelped as something struck the van, harder than any of the previous blows. She was certain this one would shatter the window.

Instead, it was followed by silence.

A moment later, someone—someone who wasn't Ying, wasn't anyone Mia recognized—called out, "Hello? Is anyone in there?"

Mia uncurled from her hiding spot. The stranger called out again, asking who was in the van. Shakily, Mia stood and ventured toward the front of the vehicle, where the windows were clear and she could peek outside. A great crack ran down the driver's side window. A flashlight beam seared through the glass, making Mia shield her eyes.

"You're safe now," said the man holding the flashlight. He lowered it a little, so Mia could see past him, where two other men had tackled Ying to the ground—were holding him there while he struggled against them. "You can come out. Unlock the door, child."

Mia hesitated. She didn't know these people. She couldn't trust them—not even if they'd seemingly come to her rescue.

The two men got Ying subdued, and one of them broke away to join the man by Mia's window. He whispered something to him: "It's all right. She'll be here in a minute."

She? Mia tensed with a shock of new, confused apprehension. Who was *She?*

And then, surging up out of the dark woods, her hair frazzled, her eyes wide, her mouth open with shock and worry, came Mia's mother.

26

IT ALL HAPPENED VERY QUICKLY AFTER THAT.
More people arrived—men and women from the nearby village, Mia assumed. Some seemed to be actual policemen. Most were just ordinary people, galvanized into a search party and driven by equal parts concern and curiosity.

Everyone kept talking all at once—to one another, and to Mia, and at Mia: "Who is this man? Were you taken? What's going on? What're you doing out here?"

After a few minutes of this, Mia's mother pulled herself together and did what she did best—she took things in hand. Right now that meant telling everyone to give them room to breathe, then asking Mia, "Where's your brother? Where's Jake?"

"With Aunt Lin," Mia said, and waited only long enough for her mother to say, bewildered, "Aunt Lin?" before telling her mother about the ring of boulders and the secret door.

Everyone galloped off again, Mia at the lead. Two of the policemen stayed with Ying, but no one else wanted to be left behind. They crashed through the woods and down the cliff, flashlights carving bright paths through the underbrush.

Soon they reached the boulders. At Mia's urging, several people got together to shove the stone door open, revealing the hidden staircase leading below. Aunt Lin and Jake's voices rang out, echoing through the tunnel: "Hello? Hello? Who's there?"

Everyone pounded down the stairs, hurried toward their voices—and stopped sharp in their tracks when they came upon the treasure room, their mouths dropping open in surprise. Everyone but Mia and her mother, who continued straight to the rest of their family.

They freed them while everyone else was still preoc-cupied with Zhu Yunwen's riches. Aunt Lin pulled Mia tight against her, and Jake embraced them both. They plied her with questions: How had she escaped Ying? Who were all these people?

But Mia had her own question first.

"How did you know?" she asked her mother. The four of them huddled there in the cavern—a spot of quiet relief among the whirl of everyone else's treasure-blind excitement. "How did you know where we were?"

Her mother bent down and hugged her again. She didn't seem able to stop hugging her. Right now Mia didn't mind at all. "We saw the firework, of course. You could see it clear to the village."

The firework. Mia had meant it as a weapon—she hadn't considered using it as a flare. Of course, she hadn't expected for anyone in the area to be looking for her either.

"But how did you know we'd come looking for Zhu Yunwen's grave?" she said.

"I found this." Her mother pulled a wrinkled piece of paper from her pocket. On it, scribbled in Mia's messy handwriting, were the English translations of Zhu Yunwen's riddles. The one leading to the grave site was at the bottom of the page. "Your uncle told me how you and Jake had been running off to places based on riddles—that you'd been looking for something. Why didn't you tell me what you were doing, Mia?"

She sounded so upset as she asked the last question that Mia didn't know how to answer.

I didn't think you'd believe me, she thought. But it didn't seem like the right thing to say. Not right now.

So she just hugged her mother back as tightly as she could and whispered, "Next time, I will."

Back in the village, all any of the residents could talk about was the discovery of Zhu Yunwen's treasure and the little girl who'd led them to it. Mia's mother let the police speak to Mia but made everyone else keep their distance. One of the officers, a soft-eyed man with a quick smile, wrote down Mia's recount of what had happened. She kept fumbling it at first, because she wasn't sure how much he wanted to know or where to begin.

"Just start at the beginning," he told her.

So she told him about the morning Aunt Lin went missing. About the letter she'd left that hadn't rung true. About the trip to Ying's house—only to discover that

Ying was missing too. She hesitated before telling him about the secret map hidden in the painting, worried that he'd laugh—or that her mother, who stood beside her with a comforting hand on Mia's shoulder, would laugh. But neither did. The officer just nodded and jotted notes as she spoke.

After Mia was finished, the policeman wanted to speak with her mother. Mia stayed for a while, but then she saw, out of the corner of her eye, two other officers pulling a handcuffed Ying toward a police car.

Mia remembered his knife at her throat. His fists pounding at the van window. Those handcuffs seemed flimsy in comparison.

She moved toward him anyway, pushed by something unspoken in her chest. She arrived at the police car just before the police did, Ying between them.

She looked at him, and he looked at her.

"Run along back to your mother," one of the officers said, not unkindly.

Mia didn't move. She had something to say—something that raged hot and angry inside her. But as she stood there struggling, it slowly ebbed away again. Turned cold and heavy.

She saw a heaviness, too, in Ying's eyes. He didn't look sorry. He didn't even look regretful. But he didn't look angry anymore, either—or filled with that wild madness that had made him so terrifying. His desperation was sad now, like a black weight in the core of his body.

Mia found words at the tip of her tongue. They weren't what she'd originally meant to say, but she spoke them anyway.

"I'm sorry," she said. "About your wife."

Before she could say more, or Ying could respond, Aunt Lin saw them and rushed over to guide Mia away from the police car.

Neither of them looked back.

There was talk of keeping Mia and her family in the town a little longer. Mostly, Mia thought, because the villagers seemed to like the excitement of having them there. But as the adrenaline of the night ebbed away, Mia wanted nothing more than to be somewhere comforting and familiar again. She could tell the rest of her family felt the same. So as soon as dawn broke over the mountainside, they all squeezed into a police car and headed back to Fuzhou.

Sometime during the trip, Mia dozed off. When she woke again, she was still in the car, Aunt Lin on her left, Jake on her right, her mother in the front seat, and she forgot, for one sleepy moment, where she was or where they were headed. But it didn't matter.

They were together, and everything was all right.

EPILOGUE

"SHE'S PEEKING," JAKE SAID. "I CAN TELL you're peeking, Mia."

"I'm not," Mia protested.

She had been, just a little. But now she squeezed her eyes properly shut, her hands stretched out, palms up, like her mother had directed. A moment later, her fingers closed around something velvety and square. A box. It was just the right size to fit in her cupped hands.

"Wait, not yet—" Aunt Lin said.

There was a little *creak*, and when Mia felt the box again, it had been opened for her.

"Let the girl look," Mia's uncle said, laughing.

"Now," Mia's mother said.

Mia opened her eyes. On the table, the recently extinguished candles on the cake still wafted smoke. Jake and Aunt Lin watched her, waiting. Her mother smiled at her across the table. A flash went off—her uncle snapping a picture.

"Why're you looking at us?" Jake said, exasperated. "Look at your present, Mia."

So Mia did.

In the velvet box lay a tiny, delicate pendant on a golden chain. The pendant was in the shape of two cranes—just like the dancing cranes on the painting that had started it all. They'd decided to leave that painting in China, instead of taking it home with them. It belonged here, along with the priceless historical treasures it had led them to.

"Do you like it?" Aunt Lin said. "We figured you ought to have something you could take back home—a keepsake of your trip."

"I love it," Mia said, and everyone smiled, even Jake.

They'd ended up staying here in Fuzhou a few more weeks than expected, while things got sorted out. Once upon a time, Mia would have thought that was the worst thing in the world. It meant she'd barely have any summer vacation left at all once she got back to the United States. It meant she had to celebrate her twelfth birthday here in China instead of with Lizbeth and Thea and their friends from school.

But right now, sitting here in this little apartment, listening to the busy street sounds below, waiting for her mother to cut the birthday cake, it didn't feel horrible at all.

The phone rang, and her uncle hurried off to answer it, waving at the others to stay where they were.

"So," her mother said, sliding the first slice of cake onto Mia's plate. "What's next for you treasure hunters in the family? Sunken Spanish gold? The lost Fabergé eggs?"

Aunt Lin grinned and slipped an arm around Mia's shoulders. The two exchanged a look.

"Oh, we don't know just yet," Aunt Lin said. "There's a lot out there. We'll have to see what tickles our fancy."

"And has the best story," Mia said.

"Very true."

"And we'll be busy for a while, anyway," Mia added.

They were still getting calls all the time asking for interviews or photo ops with regards to Zhu Yunwen's treasure. The plans for all those priceless items were still up in the air—there was talk of adding them as an exhibit at one of the major national museums, or maybe even building a new expo to put them on display near the location where they'd been hidden for more than five centuries.

Her mom laughed. Jake rolled his eyes.

Mia sat back in her chair and smiled. It would be nice to take a break for a while. But when the next adventure came, she'd be ready for it.

In the meantime, she had quite a story to tell Thea and Lizbeth once she got back home.

"Speaking of busy," her uncle said, bringing the telephone into the living room, "the call's for you and Aunt Lin. That journalist you met last week? She wants to fact-check something."

"Again?" Jake said. "How many times can she ask the same questions?"

Mia's uncle grinned and traded Mia her slice of cake for the phone. "I guess she wants to be sure about things. It's a very important story, after all."

Aunt Lin closed her bedroom door quietly and motioned for Mia to put the journalist on speakerphone. The woman's cheery voice filled the room, gliding through pleasantries before getting to the root of the call. By then the two of them were both seated on the bed, their slippers kicked off on the floor, their knees knocking into one another.

"I know it's hard to be exact about the history concerning Zhu Yunwen," the journalist said, "what happened after his supposed assassination, I mean. But I wanted to make sure I got *your* version of the story right. Could you just walk me through it again?"

"Sure," Mia said, smiling at Aunt Lin. "But we have more than one version. It might take a while."

The woman laughed. "I have all the time in the world."

Mia settled more comfortably on the bed and leaned her head against Aunt Lin's shoulder—felt Aunt Lin lean against her, too.

"You tell it," her aunt whispered.

"Well, all right," Mia said, and began.

ACKNOWLEDGMENTS

BOOKS ONLY COME TO FRUITION THROUGH THE
hard work of a great number of people, and *The Emperor's Riddle* is no exception. I have so much thanks to give to so many people—even more than can be named here:

As always, to my agent, Emmanuelle Morgen, who has been making my dreams come true since I was nineteen. And to Whitney Lee, my foreign agent, who works so hard to see my stories overseas.

To my editor, Jennifer Ung (and the rest of the amazing team at Aladdin!), who worked so tirelessly to make this book the very best it could be. Your enthusiasm was the greatest encouragement a writer could have.

To my mother and father, for taking me to and from

China so many times as a child, and for all the stories they've told me about their experiences growing up during the Chinese Cultural Revolution.

To Savannah Foley and Julie Eshbaugh, critique partners extraordinaire. And to the other lovely members of Pub(lishing) Crawl, whose support is paramount.

To Jenny Tobat and Renee Wu, for all the in-jokes and can't-even-breathe-laughter and General Ridiculousness that has kept me sane these past two years. It's been unforgettable.

(Moo).

ABOUT THE AUTHOR

KAT ZHANG LOVES TRAVELING TO PLACES BOTH real and fictional—the former have better souvenirs, but the latter allow for dragons, so it's a tough pick. A graduate of Vanderbilt University, she now spends her free time scribbling poetry, taking photographs, and climbing atop things she shouldn't. You can learn about her travels, literary and otherwise, at katzhangwriter.com.

5·17